VINDICATOR

D1553058

DOMS OF MOUNTAIN BEND

BOOK 7

BJ Wane

Editors:
Kate Richards & Nanette Sipes

Cover Design & Formatting:
Joe Dugdale (sylv.net)

PUBLISHED BY BLUE DAHLIA

DISCLAIMER

This contemporary romantic suspense contains adult themes such as power exchange and sexual scenes. Please do not read if these offend you.

DEDICATION

This book is dedicated to my awesome editors, Kate Richardson and Nanette Sipes, and my wonderful beta readers, Sandie Buckley, Gaynor Jones, and Kathy Heare Watts. Thank you so much, ladies – I couldn't do it without you!

CONTENTS

Prologue

Cheyenne, Wyoming

A bead of nervous sweat rolled down Melinda Walsh's spine, her heart still pounding from the horror of witnessing a man's brutal execution. Not just any man – the father she'd traveled from San Diego to meet for the first time. Berating herself for acting so foolish wouldn't erase the scene she'd witnessed when she'd walked into his one-man accounting office unannounced an hour ago and followed the sound of voices down a short hall to the storage room. She slammed her eyes shut against the spray of bright blood against a white wall then opened them, hearing someone enter the police captain's office where she waited to repeat her story.

Along with Captain Honeycutt, whom she'd already met, two other men entered the room, their size dwarfing the space. The red-haired detective offered a friendly smile, but it was the focused, dark-eyed perusal the other man subjected her to that, strangely enough, settled her nerves. His gaze never wavered as he removed his Stetson and took the chair across from her, his nearness somehow calming. Or maybe it was just a simple matter of female appreciation for his attractive, five-o'clock-shadowed, rugged face and broad shoulders. How did she reach the age of thirty without realizing cowboys were so much sexier than beachcombers?

"Did you find anything at the address I gave the first officer?" she managed to ask, assuming these were the detectives sent to check out her story over an hour ago.

"Yes, ma'am, we did. I'm Detective Rossi, and this is my partner, Detective Reynolds. As you probably figured, they didn't have time to clean up the storeroom. But we're familiar with that address and the man you described to our captain." He glanced at the mug shots in front of her and pointed to the one she had pulled out. "You're sure this is the man who shot your father?"

"Positive. I'll testify to it." The thought gave her the jitters, but there was no way she would let him get away with killing her father.

"His name is Anthony Cortez, and we've tried for a long time to shut down his drug-trafficking operation. If we can get him on murder one, he won't set foot out of prison." Detective Rossi leaned back, his laser-sharp gaze now both soothing and nerve-racking. "He won't take your testimony lightly. Would you be so willing to go up against him if you'd witnessed the murder of a stranger?"

Melinda reminded herself the detective didn't know her or the circumstances regarding her father's absence from her life. "My father *was* a stranger to me. I came here to rectify that." She pointed a trembling finger at Cortez's photo. "He robbed me of that chance."

Admiration shone in his dark gaze focused on her face. Under his breath, he murmured, "It was beauty killed the beast."

Melinda smiled, recognizing the movie line, wondering if he was a connoisseur of cinema trivia, the same as she. "The original *King Kong*, 1933. Are you a big-ape fan or of movies in general?"

Detective Reynolds rolled his eyes. "God, please don't get him started. He'll quote movies all day. If we're assigned to you at the safehouse, you can entertain him."

She hadn't thought of that, but, after a second's hesitation, decided she wasn't backing out, regardless of the hardship. She owed her father that much. Besides, she could think of worse ways to spend a few weeks than in close confines with the tall, rugged cowboy with the soul-penetrating looks.

Detective Rossi's look turned compassionate. "I can see you didn't realize the need to stay secluded if you did this. Do you want time to think about it, maybe talk it over with your family?"

Melinda's only family were her mother and aunt, and both would support her decision. "How long? I have to work." As much as she wanted that man to pay for his crime, she didn't want to lose her job as a hospice nurse.

"Anywhere from a month to three or four, but shouldn't be longer than that," he replied.

She nodded, knowing she couldn't live with herself if she didn't. "Make the arrangements."

****

Two months later

Nick Rossi sat behind the wheel of his Subaru Legacy, staring at the small house. Like every other home on the everyday neighborhood street at dusk, lights shone in the windows, and shadows of the residents flitted in and out of view. But only he and a handful of others were aware 1601 Briarwood Lane wasn't a regular residence. Thinking of the woman ensconced inside for the past two months, of her bravery despite the tragedy she'd witnessed, of her will to see justice done, of the stoic front she continued to show everyone who knew how afraid she really was, set his heart to hammering with pure, unadulterated lust.

He couldn't afford to label what he felt anything more than that basic emotion. That alone wasn't good for the lead detective in charge of keeping a witness safe until she testified against one of the state's most wanted criminals. Admitting to anything deeper or more meaningful could jeopardize his career, not to mention his objectivity.

Swearing at his stupidity, Nick grabbed the Chinese take-out bag, got out, and strode up the walk to the front door, conscious of the hidden cameras picking up his arrival and the silent alarm on each of the agent's phones. His partner, Mike, was already inside, arriving to take over for him tonight before he'd gone to get dinner. It would be his last meal sitting across the table from the woman he couldn't stop obsessing about. Word had come down last week the Cortez trial was moved up to tomorrow, a full month early. Good news for Melinda Walsh. He'd noticed the signs the confinement was getting to her.

If only the unease that made him think all was not right would let up, he could get on with putting this case behind him, and the woman inside. His sister used to tease him, telling him the intuitions he would get in the form of odd sensations crawling under his skin were a sixth sense. He ignored her nonsense until that strange prickling and disturbing agitation plagued him for the better part of a day when they'd been teens. When she hadn't come home from a ride, he'd gone with his father looking for her, finding her with a broken leg from a fall off her horse.

When he was in college, and the anxiety returned, he'd phoned home three times in one day to check on his parents. That evening, his mother called him to say his father was involved at the tail end of a pileup on the highway but was lucky enough to walk away unhurt. Nick hated the vague premonitions of an unspecified, potentially devastating occurrence, but, so far, had found no way to rid himself of them.

Tonight, Nick was left with no choice but to trust his fellow cops to handle any issues since the rules wouldn't allow for him to stay after spending the last week on night watch at the house. To keep everyone sharp and avoid burnout, they rotated weekly, allowing for plenty of mental and physical rest time.

He rapped on the door, the secret code only the agents assigned to cover the house were privy to, wishing Melinda Walsh was just another pretty face. His dilemma would be so much easier to handle and get over if he could say his infatuation stemmed from her stunning beauty. Drop-dead gorgeous didn't do justice to the striking contrast of her large, sky-blue eyes and wealth of wavy, long coal-black hair. Add in a flawless complexion, slim nose, and a mouth he'd kill to feel kissing his engorged cock, and the woman could turn a saint into a sinner with a look.

Nick figured he was already a sinner for lusting after her, his penance being forced to walk away tomorrow after escorting her to the courthouse, never to lay eyes on her again. No more late nights playing cards while trying to stump each other with their knowledge of movie trivia until she was too tired for worry to keep her from sleeping. No more listening to her soft voice with a wistful lilt as she spoke of the father whom she would never get to know, or seeing the hard, determined glint in her eyes when she vowed she wouldn't back out of testifying against the man who had caused her such grief. She was the only other person he'd ever met who was an avid movie buff and could match lines with the movie and name the year as well as he. During the last eight weeks, he'd been unable to trip her up, or she him, which had amused and challenged them both.

If Nick thought he could get away with it, he would take Anthony Cortez out himself and be done with it just to spare Melinda the hardship of facing him in court. He couldn't think of anything he wouldn't be willing to do for her, which was why it was a good thing their time together as detective and witness was coming to an end. If she didn't live so far away and hadn't heard her say she couldn't wait to get back home, to see her mother and aunt again and return to the job she loved, he would consider pursuing a relationship beyond this house.

The snick of opening locks cut off that

regret. The door swung open, and he entered the house, his gaze zeroing in on Melinda seated at the table playing cards with Owen, the only other agent there except his partner.

"Thanks," Nick told Mike, who stood holding the door.

"I thought you would never get back. I'm starving." Mike shut the door and engaged all the locks.

"You're always starving. Everything good here?" Nick nodded to Melinda and Owen, a senior agent who had been in law enforcement twice as long as he and Mike. They both were glad to have him added to the roster of rotating agents helping to cover Melinda.

Mike snorted. "All's quiet except these two arguing over cards."

"She cheats," Owen shot back, his wide smile revealing the lines around his eyes.

Nick tried not to react to the slow curl of Melinda's lips or the sparkle in her eyes as she laid her cards down and said with glee, "Gin."

"Damn, girl. That's three in a row. Let's eat." Owen stood and gave her long braid an affectionate tug. "If I have to lose, I can't think of anyone I'd rather go down in defeat to."

It seemed she'd wound her way into Owen's affections as effectively as she'd snuck past Nick's guard. Tomorrow couldn't come soon enough.

"I bet you say that to all the girls you play with." She grinned then slid her eyes up to him. Nick's gut clenched as he wondered how she could look so innocent and sultry at the same time. "Detective. That smells wonderful."

He set the large bag on the table and pulled out covered dishes. "Not too many like calamari."

"I like different."

Nick looked away from the interest in her blue eyes. Someone should inform her about the benefits of learning to hide her emotions. Either that or someone should knock some sense into him for finding himself so drawn to a witness under his protection.

"I do, too, but not when it comes to food." Owen popped the lid on his sesame chicken. "Can't go wrong with chicken."

"Boring." Melinda took a bite of calamari and sighed with exaggerated enjoyment, the sound going straight to Nick's cock.

"I would think after all you've been through lately, you would prefer boring." When she shot him a stricken look, he could have kicked himself for the retort. "Sorry, Melinda."

Mike raised a brow as red as his hair but, instead of commenting on Nick's rude rebuke, he smiled. "Nothing like a little spice to stir the pot, I always say."

Owen nodded toward Melinda. "You should listen to him, hon. Never met a man who enjoyed cooking as much as our Mike, except maybe you, Nick."

Nick took a seat and pointed his plastic fork at Mike. "I learned from the best."

Mike scooped up a bite of fried rice, replying, "Which is why you're the beneficiary of everything in my kitchen."

Nick lifted his iced tea glass. "Here's hoping I never inherit."

Melinda grinned, her slender shoulders relaxing, relieving Nick's guilt. Tomorrow morning, he would see the last of her, and that was a good thing since her future wasn't here, near him. She'd refused to enter witness protection, and, given Cortez's operation and employees were small time by most standards, he lacked the resources to remain a threat after incarceration. Once they escorted her to the courthouse and turned her over to the prosecutors, he could put her out of his mind and move on to the next case. Other agents were already assigned to cover her until the trial ended and a verdict rendered. Even in a medium-size city like Cheyenne, there was always another case.

Melinda scooted back from the table and stood. "I would offer to help clean up, but since it's mostly trash and I'm not allowed outside, I'll excuse myself. Tomorrow will be a long day."

They all bid her good night, but Nick thought he was the only one who noticed the fleeting sadness crossing her face, the hint of worry in her eyes. "Melinda." When she turned, he smiled and said, "Here's looking at you, kid."

Appreciation shone in her eyes when she answered, "*Casablanca*, '42. Thank you,

Nick."

He nodded, waited until she left the room, then said, "She's scared, about tomorrow and what might come of her testimony."

"She's doing the right thing, though, and she could still go into witness protection." Mike started gathering the empty cartons. "We haven't been able to get anything on Cortez in the ten years he's been running drugs through Wyoming. Now, with the massive increase of fentanyl coming in over the border, it's even more vital to take him down."

"Let's hope the risk she's taking is worth it and someone doesn't come in and take over for him. I'll be here early." He lifted his Stetson off the back of the chair and put it on, nodding to Mike and Owen.

Owen stood. "I'm more than ready to get back to my own life. I'll take the trash out, Mike. See you in the morning, Nick."

As soon as Owen slipped out the back door, Mike asked Nick, "Everything okay? You seem tense."

Mike always could read him like a book. They'd been partners for six years, and there was no one Nick trusted more. "Just uneasy. I wouldn't put anything past Cortez." That was the best explanation he could come up with.

"I hear you, but don't worry. We're secure here."

"You're wearing your tracker, right?"

Mike nodded and lifted his foot. "In the sole of my boot, same as you. Go. Get some sleep. You were up all last night."

He was, and he was bone tired but still on edge, as always when they were closing a case, but more so with his skin prickling. For the last three years, the two of them had taken to wearing trackers in their boots when on a case, a safety precaution no one else knew they were taking. It gave them each comfort to know they could locate the other without waiting around to go through channels if they ever got into a dicey situation.

"In the morning then. Night, partner."

Nick strode to the door then paused with his hand on the knob. Tomorrow, he wouldn't get the chance to say anything to Melinda, not with the number of cops arriving to aid in getting her to the courthouse. Giving in to the need to see her alone one more time, he pivoted and hurried to her room before Mike or Owen got wind of what he was doing. He didn't need their ribbing for the next few weeks when he would be trying to forget her.

Her door was open, and he paused seeing her in the chair in the corner, hastily brushing her hands over her cheeks. Even in the dim lighting, he could make out the uneasiness etched on her face as she jumped to her feet, and he closed the door to give her privacy. Dressed in jeans and an oversized sweatshirt, she shouldn't look so fucking appealing, but he never could resist a troubled woman. He was always drawn to the subs at his club who carried the most baggage, but he'd never met one he couldn't walk away from without regret after seeing to their needs.

He was already lamenting the end of his and Melinda's short acquaintance.

Nick went to her, the small bedside lamp spilling enough light to see her red-rimmed eyes clearly. "Melinda, if you're not sure..."

"I'm sure. I couldn't live with myself if I didn't." She held up the picture clutched in her hand. "This is the one and only photo of us, all I'll have of him now. I'm sorry. It just got to me, and it shouldn't. He never was a part of my life even though Mom kept him updated on me whenever they met for him to deliver child support. He dropped out of both of our lives eighteen years ago. Finally learning why helps, and I owe him for that, but it doesn't negate that hurt."

"He was a good man, did what he thought best under terrible circumstances." Nick had to admire her father for that. Too bad he hadn't trusted the cops like his daughter.

From what little they could unearth about Theo Melbourne's job as accountant for the drug dealer, he'd taken the position without knowing who he was working for. Once he had found out, he had ditched all ties to everyone he cared about, seeing that as his only option to keep them safe from his mistake. Luckily for Melinda and her mom, Theo had kept his short affair with Cara Walsh from his wife, paying Cara child support in cash when she informed him of Melinda's birth. He'd been divorced from his wife for two years and had left no record of his brief involvement with Cara when he discovered the truth about his boss after moving to Wyoming years ago.

Nick needed to get going before he caved to the desperate appeal in Melinda's eyes. She looked so sad and alone, yet the determined set to her mouth revealed the grit she possessed to see this through. "I have to go, and I doubt I'll have time to say goodbye after tonight. It's been a privilege knowing you, Melinda." He figured if he kept saying her name, he wouldn't be tempted to call her darlin' or some other endearment.

Her gaze darted to the closed door as she leaned into him. The first contact with her soft body, followed by a plea with that soft catch in her voice that never failed to turn him rock hard, proved to be his undoing.

"Nick, please." Her hands gripped his waist, as if she were hanging on by a slim thread and needed a lifeline. "Give me something else to think about tonight." She nipped his neck then licked over the pinprick, the slight sting and soft caress stripping him of his control as much as her whispered plea. *"Please."*

With a few shuffling steps, he had

her pinned against the wall, that one word blocking out all the reasons why this was a very bad idea. He didn't plan on kissing her, just getting her off so she could sleep, but her warm breath tickled his neck then she ran her tongue over his pulse, leaving him no choice. It was either cover her mouth with his or go insane with lust.

"Damn it, Melinda." He crushed her soft lips under the hard pressure of his mouth, taking advantage of her gasp to taste her tongue. Making quick work of undoing her jeans, he dove into her panties and sought her velvet heat. Finding her wet, tight pussy, he worked two fingers inside her, groaning into her mouth as her tongue returned his stroke.

Nick pulled his hand back, rubbing her clit, then thrust deep, hard enough to bring her to her toes on a low moan, repeating the plunges three times. Wrenching his mouth from hers, he breathed above her trembling lips, stared into her eyes, and whispered, "Go over, Melinda. I've got you." Taking her clit between his fingers, he milked the swollen, tender bud, stifling her cry of release with his mouth as she splintered apart.

Slick muscles clutched at his fingers with tight, rhythmic contractions, her orgasm spewing a copious amount of cream to ease his pummeling thrusts when he released her clit. She rode his hand with rapid pelvis gyrations, her fingers clutching his shoulders, nailing biting into his skin, her lips clinging to his. By the time she came down from the quick high and he pulled his mouth and hand away from her quivering body, they were both breathing heavily and perspiring, yet he couldn't force himself to let go of her, or this moment, yet.

"One more." Stepping back, he turned her to the wall and placed her hands against it with a warning. "Leave them there."

She surprised him when she nodded and agreed without hesitation. "Okay."

"I'm a fucking idiot," he muttered, reaching in front of her again to return to her pussy, squeezing one soft buttock with his other hand.

Melinda jerked against his deep, two-fingered plunge, saying on a released rush of breath, "If you are then so am I," then ended on a groan when he pressed his thumb against her anus. *"Oh God."*

Nick took her over again with a few more clit-abrading strokes while maintaining a soft pressure against her tight-puckered backside, sensing she was new to that touch and nowhere ready for penetration. He realized just what a bad idea this was when he drew out of her quivering clutches with slow hesitation based on regret. Hearing his name called out from the hall jarred him into moving faster.

"Hey, Nick! You still here?" Owen called out.

"Shit. Gotta go. Are you okay?" He hated rushing out but couldn't afford to have Owen or Mike come back here and get wind of this.

"I'm fine." Melinda dropped her hands and did her jeans up before facing him, her chest lifting with her heavy breathing.

Shaking his head, he took a step back from the tempting appeal on her face. "I'm sorry. I..."

She laid a hand over his mouth, halting his apology, her slender fingers trembling. "Don't say that, please. You can't possibly know how much I needed that, how much I appreciate all you and the others have done."

Owen and Mike's low voices echoed from the hall. "Take care, Melinda." He pivoted and went to the door but couldn't resist trading one more movie line with her. "May the Force be with you."

She giggled, the sound easing his tension. "Too easy, Rossi, but I appreciate the sentiment behind it. *Star Wars*, 1977."

Nick wished walking away was as easy.

****

The call came in at 2:05 a.m.

Nick fumbled for his phone, dread churning in his stomach. No good news came in the wee hours of night. He never should have ignored the odd sensations that, over the years, had told him something bad was going to happen.

"Rossi."

His captain spoke with urgency. "We just got an SOS from the safehouse. A team's on its way."

"So am I."

He clicked off and scrambled to dress, refusing to let the fear crawling down his spine shake him. Snatching his weapons on the run, he dashed out to his cruiser, flipped on the emergency lights and sirens, and hit the gas. Coming to a screeching halt in front of the house twelve record-breaking minutes later, he jumped out and was the first to reach Owen who lay crumpled in the open doorway.

Blood pooled under his torso and thigh, and Nick swore as he gently turned him over. Owen groaned, proof he was still alive despite the red stain covering his shoulder and chest. Other siren-wailing vehicles arrived, and he turned to wave the ambulance attendants over.

"See to him..." He paused when Owen gripped his arm with a bloody hand.

"Gone. They...took...them. Fuck, sorry... tried..."

"How many?" Nick shot out, pulling the tracking app up on his phone. He got a beep on Mike's hidden device, but nothing on the one Melinda wore, and prayed he found her with him.

"At least...six."

He squeezed Owen's hand and nodded to the paramedics then sprinted to his cruiser, waving to the SWAT team. "Follow me. I've got a bead on Reynold's tracker. They've already ditched Walsh's." Any kidnapping attempt would start with a thorough search of the witness.

Confident Owen was in good hands, Nick took off again. As he and the others neared the warehouse district, they cut their sirens and lights, relying only on the meager glow from parking lights. Mike's signals led them to the last building where they stopped and spread out, using hand signals to disperse the teams around the warehouse.

They went in quiet with guns drawn, searching every nook and cranny until Nick heard shouts followed by rapid gunfire. Sprinting forward, he burst into the largest space where crates were stacked along the walls, his sharp gaze zeroing in on both Mike and Melinda lying on the cement floor. He ran forward, heedless of the others spilling into the space as he took in their blood-soaked bodies.

"Shit, mother fucking cocksuckers," he swore, dropping to his knees in the blood pooled around Mike's head. He didn't need to search for a pulse. Swallowing his grief and fury, he moved to Melinda, his heart constricting at the knife gashes on her face, the blood seeping through her torn shirt. Despite the gravity of her injuries, relief flooded him when she opened pain-filled, shocked eyes and lifted a hand toward him.

"I..."

"We need a bus here, STAT!" he yelled as several SWAT members joined him. "Stay quiet, Melinda. We've got you."

She sobbed, shut her eyes, and turned her face away, as if she couldn't bear to look at him. He didn't blame her. They'd sworn to protect her, and they'd let her down. If she survived, she would never be the same.

Nick and two others did their best to slow the bleeding, all the while he fought to keep from looking over at Mike, from raging at the injustice of his partner's death, and working to contain his grief. The ambulance arrived, and chaos ensued after she was whisked away. None of the kidnappers survived their attack, which meant they were back to square one with taking down Cortez until Melinda was well enough to testify. *If* she survived, and *if* she would still agree to get on the stand.

His chest constricted as those possibilities went through his head. By the time Nick's captain sent him home, it was late morning, word had come down Melinda would make it, and his heart ached as he thought about the rough road ahead for both of them.

****

Trust no one.

Through the endless days of pain, those three words kept playing over and over in Melinda's head. Every time she recalled the terror of that night, she asked herself why she ever stopped following her dad's last words to her mother. For the last eighteen years, they'd lived their lives by those words, her mother taking them seriously enough to drill them into her head starting at age twelve. Her mom had reminded her of those words when Melinda told her she planned to testify against the man she'd witnessed murdering her father.

She hadn't told either of her parents about her plans to meet her father when she'd driven from San Diego to Cheyenne. It was just sheer luck that she'd entered his office that day ten weeks ago and followed the sound of voices down the only hall. She'd barely glimpsed inside the storeroom when the man holding a gun to her father's head pulled the trigger. Thank God she hadn't let shock keep her from slipping away as quietly and quickly as she could muster with her heart pounding against her chest wall and bile threatening to come up.

Now look where her attempt to do the right thing had landed her. No, wait, *looking* was the last thing she wanted to do. She reached up and ran a finger over the bandages on her face, not caring near as much about the inevitable scars as she did about being the cause of Detective Reynold's death. Honest to God, she despaired over how she would live with that on her conscience.

Melinda glanced out the glass partition

separating her from the nurse's desk, a pang squeezing her chest when she saw Detective Nick Rossi. *What is wrong with me?* She asked herself that every day when he came by to check on her and her body went into instant, heated overdrive just from seeing him.

Trust no one.

It hurt, actual physical pain, whenever she questioned if he was the one who had betrayed her location to Cortez. She hadn't needed Detective Reynolds to tell her Cortez must have a cop on his payroll once his men had stormed the safehouse. Since the thugs had killed the detective as soon as they realized the rescue team had found them, she knew it wasn't him. The same for Detective Phillips, who also had the bad luck to be assigned her protection and was shot at the house. That left Detective Rossi, and a slew of other cops who had taken turns guarding her for two months.

Her palms turned damp as she took in Nick's tall frame, remembering how he towered over her five-foot-five height as he'd pressed her against the bedroom wall.

His Stetson shielded his dark eyes, but she could still see his shadowed jawline, and his chiseled lips moving, talking to the nurse. After fourteen days and severe trauma, the memory of his hands on her, and in her, still lingered with enough impact to cause her pussy to spasm.

Her inability to forget him hurt the most. She'd naively thought refusing to talk to him, or anyone else with a badge, after giving her statement on that night, would enable her to forget him. She resented his hold on her, how she kept replaying their fun banter over movie lines while playing cards, and the way he'd teased her when he had come up with one she struggled with before answering. His admiration for her job as a hospice nurse had shone in his eyes and been reflected in his voice, warming her when she'd been so cold.

Every time Melinda wondered if he was the one who had betrayed her and his fellow cops, her first reaction was no way. His friendship with his partner and respect of the older cop, Owen, couldn't have been feigned. She told herself no one could act that well.

Regardless of her longing for all that to

DOMS OF MOUNTAIN BEND: Vindicator

be true, she wouldn't get duped into believing any of them again. They had enough to send Cortez to prison for years on drug charges without her testimony on her father's murder. That would have to be enough for them and her because she was done. With him behind bars, she could return home and resume her life without fear.

The nurse shook her head, probably telling him Melinda again refused to talk to him, then she shifted on the bed in uncomfortable awareness when he spun around and strode into her room. Gripping the sheet, she hardened her resolve not to let his presence affect her in any way, but that was easier said than done as he approached the side of the bed.

"I don't want to talk to anyone," she reminded him.

"So I've heard. Too bad. Do you remember anything else about that night you haven't told us?"

His deep voice curled her toes, and she cursed herself for being so attuned to his every sound, every move. "No. I've told you everything. They wore face coverings, came

BJ Wane

in fast after shooting Detective Phillips, and dragged us out of there. We weren't in the warehouse long before you got there."

Nick released a heavy sigh, as if he'd been holding his breath, then went to stare out the window with his back to her. His wide shoulders were ramrod straight and stiff, and she remembered the feel of those muscles bunching under her hands, how his warm breath had tickled her senses. She could learn to hate him for rendering her so vulnerable.

He spoke without turning around, his words twisting her heart. "I'm sorry for what you've suffered, Melinda. Nothing can make up for that, but I swear we'll find who's responsible." Turning, he nudged his hat back and crossed his corded arms, stretching his snug-fitting T-shirt with the Cheyenne Police logo. "I can see the doubt and mistrust on your face. It won't do any good for me to tell you I'm the same man you've enjoyed sparring with for weeks, or to tell you it wasn't me. But I am, and it wasn't. Someday soon, I hope you'll believe that. Take care."

Melinda watched Nick walk out without

replying. *Trust no one.* Not even the man who had wormed his way into her heart in such a short time.

Chapter One

Eighteen months later

Mountain Bend, Idaho

Nick released the stallion's leg, patting his shoulder to send the horse trotting around the corral. Noting the lack of a limp, he nodded. "That seems to have taken care of the problem. Call me if he starts favoring it again."

"I will, thanks." Ben Wilkins followed Nick back to his truck parked in front of Ben's house. "Send me a bill. I appreciate you coming out so quick. He's my best mount for when I patrol the mountain trails, which I'm scheduled to do this week."

Sliding behind the wheel, he faced Ben, a park ranger and one of his new friends since relocating from Cheyenne to just outside Boise. "No problem. Horses picking up stones or needing their hooves filed account for over half my business." He closed the door and leaned his arm on the open window, his gaze shifting to the stallion who looked happy at being pain-free.

Ben leaned against the truck, tilting his head as he gazed down at Nick. "Will I see you tonight at Spurs?"

Careful to put on a bland expression, he replied, "I'm bartending, so yeah, I'll be there."

Starting the engine, Nick tried not to read too much into his growing dissatisfaction with attending the private club outside of Mountain Bend. A year and a half had passed since he'd buried his partner and seen the last of the witness he'd failed to protect. Yet he still carried the pain of that botched protection detail with him every day, Mike's death and Melinda's devastating assault burdens he couldn't shed. Owen's recovery was the only good thing he'd left behind when he'd turned in his badge six months later, believing that was all he had to do to put the memories behind him after failing to discover who had betrayed them.

Time, a new career, and a different location had proven him wrong. The pain of those losses was still as acute as the day he'd said goodbye to Mike, Melinda, and his fifteen-year job on the force.

"If you don't mind me pointing out, you haven't participated much lately. Anything I can help with?" Ben asked, his tone reflecting concern.

In Nick's opinion, the best thing about being a member of a BDSM club was the close ties people developed. Those bonds were more pronounced at Spurs than at his previous club in Wyoming. Maybe because most of the members here were long-time friends, having grown up together in the small, rural community. Even so, Ben wasn't the only one who had welcomed him with open arms and made him feel at home from his first night. He wished he could return their friendship by opening up about the past issues that had kept him at arm's length, but his failure combined with heartbreak weren't things he was ready to share yet.

"No, but I appreciate the offer." He shrugged, as if the reason for his recent lapse in hooking up with a willing sub was no big deal. "Just going through a dry spell. I'll get my head back in the game soon."

"Been there, so I understand."

Nick smiled. "Speaking of hooking up, how's married life?"

Ben and Amie had tied the knot a few weeks ago, just in time to take a spring honeymoon cruise. Nick had just heard Adrian Coultrane was now planning a fall wedding. Either there was something in the air here in Idaho or something in the water, considering the number of Doms falling into wedded bliss lately.

Pleasure suffused Ben's face, his green eyes turning warm. "Love it. All it takes is the right person to change your mind about settling down."

"I guess I haven't met the right person, then. See you at Spurs."

Melinda's face popped into Nick's head as he drove, which was ridiculous given their brief, limited relationship over a year ago. He thought of those fifteen minutes in her room at the safehouse as a lapse of judgement, and the guilt over what had occurred afterward as his price to pay for that error. Making a career change and moving hadn't helped to put her or that botched assignment behind him.

At least Cortez was serving twenty years on drug charges. It rankled they couldn't get him on murder, for either Theo Melbourne or Mike Reynolds. Nick kept in touch with his former captain and the open cases he'd walked away from, but, of their witness, no one had heard since she'd left the hospital and Idaho. Since all of Cortez's henchmen were killed on the raid of the warehouse, he assumed she felt safe enough to take off without a word.

Nick gripped the steering wheel, wishing she would have talked to him before leaving. All attempts to reach her during the weeks following her disappearing act had failed. She refused to take any calls, and he finally had to respect her desire to put them and everything that had occurred since she first arrived to look up her father behind her. Shoving aside the remembered frustration of those weeks, he took in the vast countryside so similar to his home state's landscape. He'd welcomed the sight of the same mountain views beyond fields dotted with summer flowers as he'd driven from Wyoming to Idaho in anticipation of settling on his newly purchased fifty acres.

Rose and Ghost, his speckled grays, had settled into their new home without a hitch and liked the companionship of the other horses and having him around a lot more on a daily basis. Other than raising quarter horses, Nick's work as a farrier included specializing in veterinary hoof care for horses. His new career was a big change from being a detective, but the challenge had paid off. He was content with his horses and new friends, and enjoyed remodeling the fixer-upper house in his spare time.

All of which didn't explain his recent blasé attitude toward playing at Spurs. Until he could get his head back in the game, it wouldn't be fair to engage with the submissive members. At one time, he would have considered a scene with Kathie who joined for a good time and didn't take anyone seriously. But lately, Neil seemed to get a kick out of her, so he didn't intrude.

His place was in between Ben's and the small town of Mountain Bend, about two miles off the main road. He passed a herd of grazing bison and braked for a group of graceful gazelle sprinting across the road before coming to his turnoff. The similarity in landscape and wildlife to Wyoming kept him from missing home, and, with Mike gone, he didn't leave behind any other close friends. His parents had moved to South Carolina years ago, and his sister followed them with her family. As much as he enjoyed his trips to visit them, he much preferred the mountains to the coast, although sometimes, during the harsh winter, he would question the sanity of that preference.

A sense of pride always enveloped Nick when he looked out at his horses grazing in the pasture behind the stable. Parking in the carport he'd added on the side of the house last year, he got out and strode to the fence where his hired hand Spenser stood.

Nick nodded toward a chestnut mare with white forelegs. "How's she doing today?" The mustang had come to him through a wild mustang rescue in Montana after they'd treated her for a severe neck wound from an aggressive stallion. She would carry the deformed indenture in her neck for life, but at least she'd survived the brutal attack.

"Not bad, all considering." Spenser heaved a sigh. "Abuse always rankles, no matter the source. I wonder what she did to piss off the stallion." A rueful grin tugged at the corners of his mouth.

"It doesn't matter. No means no, regardless of what language or species is saying it. She's still staying to herself, I see." There were eleven other horses in the same enclosed section, but none of them ventured close to the scarred newcomer.

Spenser eyed him askance. "That's probably for the best, don't you think?"

Nick dug a piece of straw from his pocket and stuck it in his mouth, shifting it to the side to chew. "For now, but I don't want it to go on too long. She'll get set in her ways if it does and become harder to break."

"Jose was asking what will happen to her if she's too skittish to ride. He has a softer heart than most."

Nick's other cowhand was prone to babying the horses, and he'd found it amusing to hear the older man talk to them as if they were little kids.

"I would keep her, but it's an expense I don't need or want. With luck, I can turn her around, at least enough she'll make a nice pet for someone low-key." Straightening away from the rail, he pulled his Stetson brim down, saying, "I'll be in my office for a while then I'll help get them bedded down for the night before leaving again. If you need anything, holler."

"Will do, sir."

Slapping him on the back, Nick stated with force, "And cut the sir crap."

He walked away, leaving Spenser chuckling.

Entering the old farmhouse he was in the middle of remodeling, he was glad the last of the new hardwood floors were laid this week. That was one job he wouldn't mind never doing again. They looked damn good, though, even if he said so himself. The rich, dark tone kept the white walls from appearing too stark and sterile. He threw together a cold-cuts sandwich in the torn-up kitchen, about the only option left for meals until he found time to install the countertops and hook up the sink.

Carrying his dinner into the office, he settled behind the desk and caught up on paperwork while eating, or tried to anyway. He struggled to stay focused, something that had plagued him of late, along with memories of Melinda. Her stoic determination to do the right thing for the father she'd admitted had never been a part of her life had struck a chord in him. The people he usually dealt with rarely possessed such admirable traits. Still, when he saw her for the first time at the safehouse, he'd hoped he would discover the tug of attraction he'd experienced when meeting her at the precinct had been an ill-advised fluke.

Not so. Nick had found her in her room, alone in the semi-dark, sitting cross-legged on the bed playing cards. When she glanced up at him, her vivid blue eyes conveying worry before darkening with resolve, he'd felt that same damnable tug.

"*Anything you want to talk about, anything you're unsure of, uneasy over?*" Nick offered, unable to walk away when she looked so vulnerable sitting there, alone.

A rueful smile curled her soft lips. "*I wouldn't know where to begin, but thanks, I'm fine.*"

"*Solitaire in the dark?*" He entered the room, stopping at the bed to gaze down at her. "*If you're fine then you're weird.*"

"*It's a mindless game and good for passing the time. I'm not used to sitting idle, with nothing to do. That will be the hardest part about staying holed up here.*" She continued to flip cards as she spoke, her attention on the game, or so he assumed until he joined her on the bed.

Melinda's eyes flew up in surprise, the flare of something close to what he was feeling in her gaze until she masked it with a calm expression when he asked, "*Do you play gin?*"

She scooped the cards up and started shuffling. "*Gin, crazy eights, poker. You* name it, I'll play. My mom, aunt, and I spent a lot of evenings at the card table when I was growing up."

Curious, he picked up his hand and asked, "What about your father? You mentioned you came here to get to know him. You're willing to go through a lot for a man who wasn't there for you when you were younger."

She picked up and discarded before answering. "But he was. I was about two when Mom learned he was married and ended their affair. According to her, he insisted on paying child support, meeting her every month to give her enough cash to cover all my expenses, including child care so she could work. He may not have planned for a kid but never shirked his responsibilities."

Nick shuffled his cards around then discarded. "You said you'd never met, and that's why you came here in the first place."

She shrugged. "I have no memories from when I was that young, and Mom thought it best if I didn't get attached to a man who wouldn't openly claim me because *he feared his wife would find out. Mom never forgave him for that duplicity, not even when he offered to leave his wife for her. Said she could never trust him again after that. I figured that was between them; I was happy with just Mom. Gin." She laid her hand down, wearing a smug expression.*

"Two out of three." He gathered the cards and shuffled, interested in learning more. "And then he got in bed with Cortez, accepting the job out here."

"Yeah." Melinda sighed, the sound as sad as her tone when she explained, "He told Mom he didn't know who he was working for when he took the job, but when he learned and knew there was no going back, he sent her a final payment, enough to last us several years, until I turned eighteen, explaining why he had to cut all ties for our safety. His wife divorced him, and he lost everyone who mattered due to that mistake."

Nick's gut clenched as he thought of the risk and danger her trip here had put her in just so she could meet Theo. "What were you thinking, then, coming here?" he demanded.

Melinda's jaw tightened with anger,

and she flashed him a scathing look. "I don't expect anyone who grew up in a perfect family, with both parents and siblings, to understand. I felt I owed him for the sacrifices he made for us, and wanted to pay him back just a little by letting him meet me as an adult. I figured we could spend a few hours together without his boss finding out. I was wrong."

Nick swore at his inability to let go of those memories, or the strong feelings he'd developed for Melinda during those weeks of getting to know her, and he left his office without having gotten much done. Returning to the stable yard, he grabbed two leads off the fence and whistled for Ghost, his dapple/gray. The stallion came trotting up to him and Nick gave him a sugar cube then hooked reins to his bridle. Swinging up onto his back, he enjoyed the ripple of muscles under his legs as he held on by digging his thighs and knees against Ghost's sides. They both liked it when he rode bareback.

He rode into the pasture to help bring horses in for the night, a pleasant evening chore except in the dead of winter. Then it could be a frigid pain in the ass. And yet he stayed instead of following his family to a warmer climate. Glancing toward the silhouette of mountains rising into the dusky sky, he still couldn't picture himself anywhere but the West. Jose and Spenser were already each leading two mustangs toward the stables, and he lifted a hand to indicate he would help. Nick started toward the seven horses grazing near the pond then spotted his newest mare by the woods, still keeping to herself.

Nick veered toward her, deciding to get the hardest catch over first. In the week he'd had her, she hadn't warmed up to anyone, preferring to nip at any hand reaching to touch her rather than make nice. She was just as unfriendly with the other horses, turning aggressive if they came up to her then meek and skittish when one would return her nastiness with an attitude matching hers.

"Hey, girl," he crooned softly as he walked Ghost close to her. "I guess I should name you, shouldn't I?" Most times, he wouldn't name a rescue right away, depending on how long he thought it would take to rehome the horse. "How about Merry? That's my goal for you, to see you merry again."

The mare tossed her head, eyeing him with tolerance before giving Ghost the evil eye. "I wouldn't if I were you," he warned her. "He'll retaliate." She seemed to back off that risk, remaining still and docile until Nick reached forward, intending to clip the lead to her bridle. Merry made a go for his hand, but Ghost intervened and butted her nose. When she backed down, Nick grunted. "Huh, I should have thought of using you before now." He patted the stallion's neck then tried again to attach the lead, this time succeeding without Merry trying to eat his hand. "Good girl." Her ears twitched hearing the praise, her gaze less wary when she turned her large doe eyes his way again. "A little progress. You just made my day, sweetheart."

Darkness had fallen, and Nick's stomach was rumbling again by the time he bid the guys good night, locked up, and got on the road to Mountain Bend. He had enough time to grab something to eat before going to the club and texted Neil Pollono to meet him at the Watering Hole. With over half of the club members now in committed relationships, it was harder to find someone available for a last-minute invitation to get together. Neil was one of the few who, like Nick, harbored no plans for going down that road.

Nick wasn't opposed to settling down, but, at the age of forty, he figured if he hadn't met the right woman by now, the odds were against doing so. Neil, on the other hand, swore he was content remaining single and playing the field, even if he seemed to be focusing on one sub at Spurs the last few months.

The town of Mountain Bend was significantly smaller than Cheyenne, but it hadn't taken Nick long to discover the draw of the little community where everybody knew everyone's business. He parked in front of the bar the same time Neil pulled in, and Nick got out to greet him. "Thanks for joining me."

"Your timing was perfect. I just clocked out and was debating on whether to pick up something or suffer through my own cooking again." Neil's blue eyes were mere slits against the sun as he removed his Stetson.

"Busy day?" Nick held the door then followed Neil inside and gestured toward an empty table.

"Hunting season is always busy dealing with lost groups or individuals and violators of the state's public park's rules. There are few cabins left for rent, from what I've heard. I'll take a beer," Neil told the young waitress who came over with menus.

"Make that two." When she walked toward the bar, Nick said, "I just sold a few horses to the dude ranch. Bo Hopkins said they had expanded their trail rides to accommodate the number of reservations coming in. Good for business all around."

"But harder on Ben and I and the others," Neil returned with a dry smile, removing his hat to lay it on the table. "Dakota just worked with us in locating that missing teen. Hell of a tracker. He found her in less than an hour after we'd searched for over four." With a rueful look, he tunneled his fingers through his dark-brown hair.

Nick grimaced, recalling the missing teen cases he'd worked to solve. "Anything involving kids is tough. At least you had a good ending." Unlike his last case. He tried not to let himself wonder how Melinda had been coping with her scars, a constant reminder of her ordeal. He couldn't blame her for refusing to testify after that, but the frustration of having to drop that murder case still rankled. At least they had enough on Cortez to get him on the drug charges.

"Yeah, I agree. We suffered through one several years ago that didn't end well, the kid having drowned in one of the creeks. But let's order and talk about something more pleasant," Neil said when the waitress returned with their drinks.

"Good idea." They both got the chicken club then Nick couldn't help asking, "So, are you hooking up with Kathie again or someone else for a change?"

"It depends on if she pisses me off."

Nick chuckled. "I thought that was a given with her."

"Yeah." Neil sighed and shook his head. "I either want to strangle her or fuck her. There doesn't seem to be anything in between with that girl."

"Ah, well, she's young. Isn't that the

draw, her youth and free spirit?" he asked, cocking his head.

"Not her age. I don't usually go for the younger ones."

Nick grinned. "But?"

Neil shrugged with a sheepish look. "But there's something about her antics that keeps tugging me back to her. She's fun."

"There's definitely nothing wrong with fun." In fact, he wished he could get back into the fun of hanging out at Spurs. But that damnable itch that started weeks ago wouldn't let up enough for him to get interested in playing again.

Nick was still in wishful thinking mode two hours later, manning the bar at Spurs while he took in the scenes with voyeuristic appreciation but little interest in participating. He liked the rustic look of the renovated log structure, the beams adorning the high ceiling, dark hardwood floors, and the hay bales stacked along the wall near a secluded alcove notched out for semi-privacy. The recent addition of an upper floor with private rooms was met with approval by everyone, and he wouldn't mind trying out the new bondage bed if he ever found an interested partner.

His gaze shifted to Clayton, the county prosecutor, who had his pretty wife, Skye, dangling at a chain station, her pale body flushed and writhing as he applied his flogger again. He recalled the last time he had used the chain, binding Charlotte's lush body then enjoying her moans as he tormented her with a mini spanker. He loved snapping those small leather squares on lily-white flesh and watching the tender skin turn pink. Neil's frustrated voice drew Nick's gaze toward the front doors where his friend looked to be having an intense conversation with Kathie. Nick wondered at his displeased expression, but Dakota and his wife, Poppy, stepped up to the bar, pulling his attention away from speculating on Neil's problem with his girl.

"What can I get you two?" he asked, enjoying the sight of Poppy's long legs below the clinging sheath she wore. He just wished her blue eyes didn't remind him so vividly of Melinda's.

"Two brews." Dakota wrapped a thick arm around Poppy's waist and held her back against his chest.

Poppy's slim, red brows dipped in a frown. "What if I don't want a beer?"

"You do," her husband returned, his tone implacable.

Nick didn't say anything when she rolled her eyes, figuring it wasn't his place. "Coming right up." He reached into the cooler and grabbed two bottles, a stab of envy poking his gut watching the two of them. In the short time he'd been here, he'd witnessed several friends commit to their significant others. Having reached middle age without finding that one person he could settle down and be happy with, he figured marriage wasn't in the cards for him. That hadn't bothered him until witnessing the pleasure his friends were reaping from their spouses, several even more so with their impending fatherhood.

Shake it off, Rossi.

Easier said than done, but he managed to paste on a sincere expression when he handed over their drinks. "I hear your tracking skills were instrumental in locating a missing girl recently. Nice going," he told Dakota.

Poppy lowered her beer and glared at her husband. "You didn't tell me that."

Dakota scowled at Nick before addressing his wife. "I told you I was helping with the search party and that we found her. It was no big deal."

"Hey, I have bragging rights, don't I, Master Nick?" She flashed him an impish grin, her face softening as Dakota tightened his arm and pulled her closer.

Nick ignored the pang Poppy's contented expression gave him, recalling the same look on Melinda's face without even trying. He shouldn't be able to remember any minute details about a witness after all this time, and he kept questioning why lately he couldn't stop thinking about her.

Raising his hands, palms up, he tried joking to get himself in a better mood. "Keep me out of it. I don't get involved in domestic disputes. I'll catch you later." He knew when to retreat and moved down the bar, spotting Neil appearing none too happy.

"Your mood seems to have changed. What gives?" Nick braced his hands on the bar top in front of Neil.

"Women." A hint of disgust colored Neil's tone. "Whiskey, straight. Please," he tacked on.

Grabbing a glass off the shelf behind him, Nick set it down and filled it halfway. He slid it over to his friend, waiting for him to take a hefty swallow and answer.

"Kathie just stopped by to tell me she's hooked up with a guy, a *vanilla* guy." Neil shook his head, as if he couldn't wrap his mind around her reasoning. "She says she won't be back."

Nick cocked his head. "I didn't realize you were serious about her. I'm sorry."

Neil scowled and took another drink. "I'm not, but I don't want to see her make a mistake. She's not cut out for a vanilla relationship. What the hell is she thinking?"

"Who knows? Maybe she needs a change. She was young when she started here, from the little I know." He couldn't picture the one sub who got off pushing Doms' buttons going for a steady, non-kink relationship, but he didn't know her all that well. Kathie had seemed happy playing with Neil in the past months, but the girl was flighty, something

Neil should have remembered.

"She's still young, and naïve. Her choice." Neil downed the last swallow of his drink and handed him the empty glass. "Time to make the rounds for a change. Thanks."

"Have fun."

Nick watched him saunter toward the seating area where the unattached members liked to congregate, wondering when Neil would realize Kathie had managed to get under his skin. *None of my business,* he thought, especially since he had his own issues to sort out.

His shift bartending ended two hours later, and he turned the job over to Clayton, planning to leave until Charlotte bounced up with a beaming smile. Leaning across the bar top, she wrapped her fingers around his wrist, the thin strap on her silky camisole slipping far enough to expose one plump breast and rosy nipple.

Unabashed by both Clayton's and his gazes, she spoke in a wheedling tone. "Come dance with me, Master Nick. Pretty please."

Clayton nudged him with his elbow, lifting one brow, his blue eyes twinkling.

"C'mon, Master Nick, dance with the poor girl. She asked nicely."

Nick frowned at Charlotte. "You know I prefer doing the asking."

He'd never cared for overtures from women, even if that did make him sound chauvinistic. Unbidden, a pair of pleading, desperation-filled blue eyes popped into his head, another soft voice pleading with him. Damn it, that sealed his decision. He would do just about anything to stop the memories of that night from popping up.

"But I'll make an exception this time." He sent Clayton a warning look. "Not another word out of you."

Clayton's grin flashed. "Wouldn't think of it. Go on, I've got this."

"Thanks." Nick came around from behind the bar and clasped Charlotte's hand. When he noticed she'd righted her strap, he reached up and lowered it to her elbow again, baring her breast. "I like it better that way." If she hadn't cared in front of him and Clayton, it shouldn't bother her in front of anyone else.

She turned pink but smiled. "You're the

boss."

"Yep."

A slow number was playing by the time they reached the dance floor, and he pulled her into his arms. Her soft breasts pressed against his chest, her nipples already hard pinpoints. Nick kept hold of her hand and slid his other arm around her waist, his hand down to her curvy ass to palm one plump cheek.

"I'm glad you haven't lost weight, sweetheart. I like your curves." Last time they had gotten together, she'd sworn she was going on a diet.

Charlotte chuckled, her brown eyes crinkling in the corners. "I tried, all of three days. Giving up food, any food, isn't going to happen."

She was round and soft but not overweight, either by his or most men's standards. "Good. Tell me what you've been up to."

She rambled on about her dissatisfaction with her job as a receptionist at the health clinic followed by an argument she'd had with her sister. He tuned her out for the most part, trying to concentrate on the slow sway of their bodies together and grinding his pelvis against hers. His cock stirred, making it into a semi-erection despite the tight confines of his jeans, which was always a good signal. But his big head refused to go along, even when he slid inside her panties and dug his fingers into one fleshy buttock.

Charlotte's low moan wasn't the sound his head registered, her breathy sigh against his neck not the warm sensation he kept thinking about. Cursing the sixth sense, or whatever other nonsense label others might attach to the unease he'd been experiencing lately, he pulled away from her as soon as the song ended.

"I'm sorry, Charlotte." Nick slid the strap back up over her shoulder after brushing his thumb across her puckered tip. "I'm beat tonight and heading out. I'll look you up next time." He escorted her off the dance floor then gave her a lingering kiss.

"I'll take you up on that offer, Sir. Thanks for the dance."

"You're welcome."

Nick waited until she joined a small

group and Master Simon put his arm around her. He was a stricter Dom than Charlotte normally went for but could be trusted with someone not into the harsher side of BDSM.

Spinning on his heel, he strode toward the foyer, nodding at Neil who had found someone to torment on the St. Andrew's cross. Nick wished he could control his exasperation with his thoughts as easily as Neil seemed to set aside his displeasure with Kathie.

Chapter Two

"There you go, Mr. Fairfax. Are you comfortable?"

Melinda smiled down at her patient, noting the shallow breathing. He didn't have long now, maybe a day or two. As a hospice nurse, she'd learned most patients didn't fear the inevitable but embraced it. Many told her death would be a welcome alternative to their suffering, those of strong faith saying they looked forward to being whole and healthy again, and in a better place.

"As comfortable as I can be." He reached out with a gnarled hand and patted her arm. "You're a good girl, Melinda, and a godsend."

"I'm glad you think so. Get some rest, and I'll be back tomorrow. Sarah is here."

He drifted off, and she left his room to

greet Sarah, the second-shift nurse, in Mr. Fairfax's small living room, where she was conversing with Tim Fairfax, her patient's son.

"He's sleeping and shouldn't have any issues tonight. Doctor Livingston upped his meds," she told them.

Melinda suffered along with her patients when their bodies were riddled with a painful disease. In the two weeks she'd been assigned this case, she'd gotten to know Tim, and that he was sad for his father's impending death but relieved he wouldn't suffer for much longer.

"That's good," he replied. "I'll let you two talk then walk you out, Melinda."

Sarah waited until Tim went into the kitchen before saying, "It's hard on him."

"It always is on family, at least devoted family." Melinda handed her the updated medical chart. "Here you go. I'll see you in the morning."

She took the file. "Thanks, Melinda. Have a good night."

"You, too."

It had been so long since she'd enjoyed

a decent night's sleep, but no one knew that except her mother. Not since witnessing her father's murder had she slept the night through or without disturbing dreams keeping her from getting sufficient rest with one exception. The night Detective Rossi had left her body vibrating from those off-the-charts orgasms, she'd slept better than she'd had in the two months prior. She was thirty at the time, and he wasn't the first man to touch her, so why couldn't she forget him or that final farewell?

Melinda had struggled with that question since returning home, but at least she was free to continue living her life, unlike Detective Reynolds. His death haunted her, the guilt difficult to live with. She regretted failing to testify against his murderer as much as denying her father justice. After the sacrifices Theo had made to keep her and her mother safe when he wasn't even a regular part of their lives, his killer deserved life in prison for his murder, not just twenty years for drugs.

Regrets wouldn't keep her safe, however, and the failure of law enforcement in Wyoming to discover the mole in the Cheyenne police department would continue to prevent her from testifying. The first six months after she'd left the hospital and returned home, she'd kept in touch with Captain Honeycutt, the detective's boss. Disgusted with his same reply of nothing yet every time she inquired about the leak, she'd quit calling. The stress of knowing the person who had betrayed her and his fellow police officers, especially not knowing if it was Nick, had been getting to her to the point her only option was to cut ties with that department altogether. It hurt too much to think the detective she'd enjoyed such a special rapport with could have deceived her and his partner.

"Ready?" Tim asked, meeting Melinda at the front door.

"Yes, but you know you don't have to walk me to the curb. You live in a very safe neighborhood," she replied as he held the door open and she stepped outside.

"My dad ingrained polite manners in me." His lined face reflected sadness before he smiled. "I've done the same with my boys."

Walking down the drive to her car, she

sent him a rueful grin. "Your boys are in their forties." When they reached the curb, she squeezed his arm as he opened the door for her. "Your dad is lucky to have lived to see his great-grandchildren grow up."

"I know, and we're lucky to have you and Sarah here, easing his last few days. See you in the morning."

"Good night, Tim." She slid behind the wheel and drove home, bemoaning the amount of traffic that never seemed to let up, no matter what time of day. Melinda supposed that was only one of the prices to pay for living in an area with such nice weather year-round and close proximity to several beaches.

Working twelve-hour shifts didn't leave much time for other activities until her next day off, so when her phone buzzed the minute she entered her apartment, she wasn't happy at the delay in getting dinner. She was even less pleased when she saw the call was from Captain Honeycutt. Eight months had passed since they'd last spoken, and her first thought was for Detective Rossi, the memory of those intense orgasms he'd gifted her with never having faded in all that time.

Her heart slammed against her chest as she stared at his number and name on the caller ID Was he getting in touch again to tell her they'd found their backstabbing mole? She couldn't think of another reason for him to contact her after all this time, not when she'd left them with no doubt about her refusal to testify after that horrible night. If so, *would* she return to take the stand against the man who had caused such pain for her and her mother?

"I won't know until I answer," Melinda muttered, leaning against the door. She brought the phone to her ear and sucked in a deep breath. "Captain. What can I do for you?" She was quite proud of her calm, neutral tone in the face of her churning anxiety.

"Melinda, how are you?" His friendly voice failed to warm her.

"I'm good." Not willing to drag this out, she asked, "What's happened?"

Honeycutt's heavy sigh came through the line and put her on edge. "I'm sorry. Cortez has been released on a technicality.

The DA tried but was unable to persuade the judge to change his mind. Our only option is to have you testify about the murder."

A ball of nausea traveled from her stomach to her throat. The drug dealer had been a small-time pusher compared to the players in control of the bigger networks in the country, and all six of his henchmen were killed in the raid on the warehouse during her rescue. But he'd proven how vindictive he could be when he'd killed her father who had worked for him for over fifteen years, his reason for doing so still a mystery to her.

"Not unless you've found out who leaked the location of my whereabouts last time," she returned. No way would she trust anyone in that precinct again until the person responsible for Detective Reynold's death and Detective Phillips' injuries, let alone her pain and suffering, was found.

"We haven't, but we won't give up trying. We'll keep you safe, Melinda, I promise."

"Yeah, right. That's what you said last time." Pushing away from the door, she paced her compact living room. "I'm not risking it."

"He knows who you are now. Even with

his men dead, he can come after you, either himself or hire someone. You'll always be a threat since there's no time limit on the murder charge."

Trust no one. Her mother had drilled that into her following her father's warning to her, yet Melinda couldn't seem to help herself whenever she thought of one person. Pausing in her pacing, she gripped the phone tighter and asked in a taut voice, "What does Detective Rossi think?"

The captain paused before answering. "He turned in his badge over a year ago and moved away. I don't know where but do know his family had relocated to South Carolina. Maybe he joined them there, but I haven't heard from him since. I have other detectives though, just as good, and whom I trust. And we're working on getting Cortez back in prison with what we have."

Better the devil you know. Nick should be the one person she suspected the most of betraying her, and it hurt to believe all those nights he'd spent laughing with and teasing her were a lie. How could he have come to her before leaving the safehouse that night, touched her the way he had, his voice rough with concern and caring, then turned around and pulled a Judas on not only her but his partner and best friend? Swimming in a sea of shock and pain, she vaguely recalled his face etched with sorrow and fury as he'd bent over her in that warehouse, the damp sheen coating his dark eyes after he'd checked Mike Reynold's condition. Was he that good an actor, or was he the only one she could trust again?

"Thanks, but no thanks," she told Captain Honeycutt, hardening her resolve. "Where is Cortez now?" Just saying the man's name made her skin crawl, the scene she'd walked in on forever etched into her head. She would never forget his look of satisfaction when he pulled the trigger against the back of her father's head, coldly ignoring his weeping pleas.

"We have a detail watching him, but his lawyer will get a judge to order us off any day, which means you could already be in danger. We have no right to keep track of him but wanted to try. He's free now and can go anywhere. We won't give up until we can get him back behind bars, which we're diligently working on, but in the meantime, is there anything I can say or do to change your mind?"

"Yes, call back and tell me you've unearthed your mole and it's safe for me to trust your department. Until then, don't contact me again."

Melinda hung up before he could respond, not wanting to hear anything else. One thing was clear, she couldn't stay here, sitting around waiting for Cortez to show up. Luckily, her mother had married a few months ago and was now off on a delayed honeymoon, cruising the Mediterranean. They would be gone for another two weeks and, with her new name, her mother would stay safe from Cortez. Melinda was the one he wanted, anyway, the only person who stood between him and a life in prison. She shuddered just from thinking that.

She put together a salad, using as many refrigerated items as possible while going over her options. By the time she finished eating, she'd decided an extended camping trip was in order. Every year growing up, she, her mother, and her grandparents would take a long vacation in the mountains. Those trips left her with fond memories of fishing and hunting with her grandfather, all four of them taking trail rides, canoeing, and riding ATVs, and cooking fresh-caught small game over an open fire. It had been years since she'd gone, but Melinda was confident she could rough it on her own until either Cortez was back in jail or she found someone she could trust with her safety. She still owned a hunting rifle but had never aimed it at anything larger than a pheasant, and then only for food. Buying fish already cleaned and gutted had become much more appealing since she'd last gone fishing, but it wouldn't bother her to catch and prepare her own again.

After she ate, Melinda made a list of necessities and things to do before she took off, keeping in mind she would have to cover her tracks as much as someone who hadn't a clue about such things could. It saddened her to bail on Mr. Fairfax after only one more day of care, but she couldn't risk hanging around any longer than that and would put in for an extended leave of absence in the morning. It would take a chunk out of her savings to finance a long getaway, but thanks to her mother's generosity in sharing her family inheritance with Melinda, she could afford the expenses.

She spent a restless night fearing Cortez coming after her and despairing of getting her life back again, and awoke angry over being forced into hiding. Once she honed her shooting skills, she swore she wouldn't hesitate to turn her rifle on him if he found her, even if the thought of aiming at a person caused her grief. Melinda dressed in her uniform then looked into the bathroom mirror at the faint, white scars marring her forehead, cheek, and neck. There were others on her chest and one on her arm, all barely noticeable unless someone got close to her.

In the last year and a half, Melinda hadn't sought or welcomed any intimacy in her life, not because she fretted over others' reaction to those signs of her ordeal. No, she didn't care about the faint scars, not when there were losses so much more important and devastating. The grief and worry she'd caused her mother by making that trip to meet the man who had fathered her, witnessing his brutal, shocking murder, and Cortez's luck in escaping justice were consequences she would have to live with for the rest of her life.

Meeting Nick Rossi, letting herself care about him more than was wise, then losing their connection completely that night topped her list of regrets.

If she were honest with herself, that loss was the one that had kept her aloof from other relationships, constantly wondering if he'd been the one to betray her and his fellow cops causing her the deepest pain. As she turned in her request for a leave of absence then spent her last day with Mr. Fairfax, unable to tell him the real reason she wouldn't be back, her resentment against Cortez and whoever in that precinct had turned traitor increased.

Even though she was exhausted by the time she got off work, she stopped at the store to stock up on food to take with her to the secluded cabin she'd booked in the Boise Mountains. Having never been there during those family trips, exploring a new area gave her something to look forward to. Maybe, if she met up with a rugged, appealing cowboy or two, she would quit thinking about and fantasizing over Nick. After all this time, she could still vividly recall her immediate damp response whenever he came through the safehouse door with his Stetson tipped low, a dress shirt tucked into his snug jeans, the sleeves rolled up to reveal his corded forearms, and the shoulder seams stretched taut. Scuffed cowboy boots finished the lust-inspiring ensemble, and when he tossed her one of his quick grins or nudged his hat up to reveal his warm, chocolate gaze, she would melt inside.

Melinda returned home, sighing as she thought of the one man she would give anything to trust again. It was a good thing he'd left Wyoming and no one knew where he'd relocated. If he were that close, the stress of staying secluded until Cortez was back in prison might tempt her to contact him. She wasn't about to go through all this trouble and effort to take a risk like that.

After bringing in the groceries she hoped would hold her for a while, she went into the garage to start up the nineteen-year-old

Jeep Wrangler her mother inherited from her grandfather. The vehicle still registered under his name and was yet another thing she believed she didn't need to concern herself over since it couldn't be traced back to her as long as she didn't get pulled over.

Tonight, she would map out her route, avoiding the main highways as much as possible, and be ready to leave first thing in the morning. Melinda prayed it wouldn't be for long. Having her life disrupted twice in such a short time was two times too many.

****

By taking back roads and staying at out-of-the-way motels, paying cash, it took Melinda three days to reach the secluded cabin she'd rented in Idaho for the next month. She groaned getting out of the Jeep, her stiff muscles proof she'd gotten soft in the years since she and her mother had driven the old vehicle on such rough roads as they'd traveled to a camping destination. Had it really been ten years, right after she'd graduated nursing school, when they'd last taken a trip together? After everything that had happened when she'd decided to look up her father, she now regretted that lapse. She and her mother had always enjoyed a close relationship, and that hadn't changed with Cara's recent marriage.

Melinda took in the small, rustic cabin with the two rocking chairs on the front porch, the flutter of birds in the surrounding trees, and the faint gurgle of a nearby rushing stream, the only sounds interrupting the peaceful silence of the woods. It was the picturesque setting of most of their campsites, and her heart twisted as she prayed for Cortez's quick reincarceration on whatever Captain Honeycutt could get on him. The isolation and aloneness were already pressing down on her, something she never felt when vacationing with her mom.

Grabbing the keys she'd picked up at the rental office, along with a map to the cabin, she went inside carrying her two suitcases. She loved the charm of the stone fireplace and old-fashioned quilt covering the double bed on the opposite wall. There were minimal green cabinets in the kitchen, but she spotted the door of the pantry described on the website that would hold the nonperishables she brought with her.

Melinda spent what was left of the day unpacking, making a sandwich for dinner, and then curled up with her reader until she turned in with an unaccustomed bout of homesickness and regret weighing her down. She awoke refreshed, the scent of pine wafting in through the open window tickling her nose, and a renewed determination to make the best of this situation replacing her despondency of last night. After scrambling eggs for breakfast, she pulled out the map of trails in the area and set out to go hiking. In a few days, once she built her stamina up again, she intended to take a trail ride, looking forward to getting on a horse again.

Over the next few days, she explored the surrounding trails, relaxing at the stream and fishing at the end of each day. On the third day, her legs were so achy, she stuck around the cabin and practiced shooting at the empty cans of food she'd eaten. It didn't take long for her to admit she couldn't hit the broadside of a barn, let alone a moving target, like a pheasant or Cortez. That last thought made her cringe, and, if she were honest, she would admit how abhorrent she found the idea of shooting a person.

But if it came down to him or her, she would do what was necessary.

The isolation was getting to her by the next day, and Melinda drove to the nearest trail-ride-excursion office, looking forward to being around people as much as she was to riding. She didn't mind the solitude as much as the unease that consumed her once night fell. That was when she realized how alone she was in keeping herself safe. Each night, she managed to get to sleep by telling herself the camp office was a short, ten-minute drive away, stables for trail rides within ten minutes of the office, and a little farther lay the closest town, Mountain Bend, which she looked forward to visiting.

Excitement hummed through her as Melinda parked in the lot in front of the stables and saw a small group of people checking in and a row of saddled horses ready to take them along a mountain ridge. With luck, today's excursion would put her in touch with some neighboring campers she could make friends with.

****

Nick straightened, dropping the mare's foreleg then patting her rump. "Last one," he told Josie, the stable manager at Chisolm Riding Stables. He had a standing monthly appointment with several clients to keep their equines' hooves trimmed and cleaned. "This one is a sweetheart." The palomino nudged his shoulder, and he chuckled, withdrawing a sugar cube from his pocket. "A sweetheart with a good memory." Holding his hand out flat, he fed her the treat then picked up his tool bag.

"They all love you. You have a way with them. Must be that sexy voice." Josie elbowed him with a wicked grin. "I bet all the younger girls fall for you as easily as the four-legged species."

"But not you?" he asked, settling his hat on his head as they walked around the barn to the front.

"Ha!" she scoffed with a roll of her eyes. "I'm too old for you to flirt with, and too married."

"I don't discriminate with age, but I also don't cross certain lines." Josie was an attractive woman in her fifties, her physical job of tending to the horses, he imagined, helping her to keep in such good shape. "Your husband is a lucky man."

"That's what I keep telling him."

Midmorning and the day was already warming up to a pleasant temperature for a long ride. Nick was thinking of doing just that when he returned to his place until his gaze was snagged by a dark-haired woman getting out of an older-model Jeep. *No way,* he thought, his heart jackhammering as he halted in his tracks and squinted to get a better look. She was the same height as Melinda Walsh, same long black braid hanging down her back, and her profile revealed a small, slender nose. From this distance and only a side view, he couldn't be sure, and logic told him it was impossible. He also knew nothing was impossible, and her presence in the area could explain the disturbing, recent prickles of awareness plaguing him.

Pointing her out, he asked Josie, "Do

you know who that is, her name? She looks familiar."

She shook her head. "I don't spend much time in the office, and I'm not familiar with the visitors. Ask Tuck; he'll know. Catch you next month."

"Sure, thanks," he returned absently, unable to pull his attention off the woman now mounting one of the horses saddled for the ride.

Odds were she wasn't Melinda, but just seeing someone who closely resembled the witness he'd failed to protect conjured up memories of those eight weeks they'd spent together. She'd managed to get under his skin as no other woman ever had, and the way his heart slammed against his chest the minute he saw this woman proved he hadn't put their association behind him. He kept his eyes on her as the guide got them arranged in single file, her quick smile as she patted her horse giving him another jolt of familiarity.

Swearing, he stashed his tools in his truck as they rode out and then strode into the office to look for Tuck, the owner. He found him behind the desk, at the computer.

"Hey there, Rossi. All done for this trip?"

"Yep, and everything looks good. You know I was a cop in Cheyenne, right?" he reminded him.

"Yeah, I remember." Tuck frowned. "Why?"

This was tricky. He had no legal grounds or authority to get information from Tuck, so went with as much honesty as he could without giving her privacy away. "I thought I recognized someone on the trail ride that just left, someone I worked with on a case. How would you feel about letting me look at your registrations?"

"I'm sorry, I can't, but give me her name, and I'll tell you if she's on there."

"Melinda Walsh." He hoped it would be that easy, but Tuck shook his head.

"Sorry, no Melinda Walsh."

"No problem. I appreciate you checking. See you in a month."

If Nick had the time, he would return when the group was expected back, just to make sure. Instead, he would have to settle for his imagination running away with him.

****

Melinda's damp palms kept slipping on the reins, her pulse still erratic from glimpsing a man who looked like Detective Nick Rossi. Same dark hair curling around his nape, same tall, muscular build, same sexy, loose-limbed stride. She gave herself a mental headshake, swaying with her mount's movements, and tried focusing on the scenery as they rode toward a mountain ridge. The guide paused to point out a moose and her offspring getting a drink at a shimmering lake still a mile away from their group. The cloudless blue sky and bright sun aided in enhancing the view of pine-covered, snow-capped mountains beyond the wide expanse of green grassland brightened with colorful summer flowers.

Yet, as they resumed riding, all she could think about was the look-alike cowboy she'd glimpsed in the parking lot. Even knowing it couldn't have been Nick hadn't prevented a pang of remembrance about his caring friendship for those two months, or her longing for more from the detective who had sworn to protect her. She shoved aside those intruding thoughts, accepting the futility of wishful thinking, and focused on the ride up a mountain trail.

They stopped at a clearing with picnic tables and took a break to eat the lunch provided by the stable. After visiting with the other guests, she learned none of them were camping near her cabin. Melinda thought that news would be good since she'd started this with the intention of staying off the grid to keep Cortez from finding her, but all it did was emphasize the loneliness that came with the necessary isolation. As much as she enjoyed the outing, she returned to the cabin later that afternoon tired, a little sore, and questioning her sanity when all she could think about was the stranger who reminded her of Detective Rossi.

"Get over him, already," she muttered, tossing her purse on the sofa then making her way into the bathroom. Looking into the mirror above the sink, she ran a finger down the thin white line marring her right cheek, the terror and pain of her ordeal rushing back to torment her. She could still hear the same man who had been there when Cortez shot her father, his voice taunting her as he ran a knife down her face then over her forehead. Poor Detective Reynolds, Mike, had struggled against the hold of two other men, cursing them, his eyes pleading with her for forgiveness.

Forgiveness for what – failing to protect her or betraying her? She still didn't know but continued to question how he, Nick, or Owen could have done such a thing after all those weeks of giving her their friendship on top of their undivided, caring protection. If not one of them, then someone close enough to her case to find out where she was.

None of her scars were delivered with as much pain as watching those thugs murder Mike. Melinda found living with that guilt, knowing if it weren't for her, he would still be alive, the hardest thing to cope with since going in search of her father.

Turning from the mirror, she swore she wouldn't hesitate to pull the trigger if Cortez found her.

.

Chapter Three

66What are you cooking tonight?"

Melinda looked up from her chopping, her stomach flip-flopping at Detective Rossi's nearness. She'd heard him come in, her pulse jumping listening to his deep voice as he spoke with Detective Philips. Every time Nick had given her one of those intense perusals this week, as if he were trying to read into her mind, her unease had lessened. The other two detectives were nice, but he always took that extra step that did so much to settle her nerves.

"Fajita chicken salad. Homemade dressing and tortilla chips."

Those sexy lips curled at the corners, just enough to soften his hard face and make her wish they'd met under different circumstances. "Do you honestly think a salad will fill up three men?"

"No, that's why there's a chocolate cheesecake in the refrigerator. Here." She handed him the knife. "You finish chopping the broccoli and cauliflower while I work on the radishes and carrots." He'd surprised her the other night when he'd cooked for everyone, the lasagna the best she'd ever eaten. Cooking was another thing they had in common, along with their fixation on movies.

As if reading her mind, he took the knife, saying, "A movie trivia buff and a great cook. I couldn't ask for a more compatible witness to protect."

Melinda's fingers tingled where he'd brushed them with his. She turned her attention to the vegetables and worked to get herself under control. He was good at his job; that's all there was to the attention he gave her.

"It's not a banquet, but I promise you'll like both. At least the recipes were hits with my family."

He nudged her with his elbow. "Life is a banquet, and most poor suckers are starving to death!"

She laughed at his attempt to mimic Rosalind Russell's voice. "Auntie Mame, uh...'56, '57? And you make a terrible Rosalind."

"Gotcha. 1958."

"Are you sure?"

Pleasure swept through her when he replied, "We'll look it up after dinner."

Melinda rolled out of bed, wishing she could put those memories behind her, and figured it was the glimpse of someone who looked like Nick that prompted that dream. She showered and dressed, more than ready to spend time around people after the last days of isolation. When she'd come up with this idea, she'd planned using her memories of previous camping trips and hadn't counted on the loneliness of going it alone. With luck, the day trip to the small, historic town of Mountain Bend and a tour of the 1880s mining town along the river would pick up her spirits.

It was midmorning when she reached Mountain Bend, and she took her time driving the streets slowly, noticing the plaques on the renovated city office buildings that dated them back to the turn of the century. Rounding the corner, she passed the library and a small park where a young couple was having lunch at a picnic table. Pulling into a vacant spot, she took in the quaint shops lining the street, glad to see she wouldn't stand out as a tourist, considering the number of people strolling the boardwalks.

An hour later, her arms laden with her purchases, she reached the candle shop, the place she'd saved for last. At home, her apartment was filled with candles she rotated burning, having yet to come across one with a scent she didn't like. Picking up a few for the cabin would make it seem more like home. She stored her bags in the Jeep and then stepped inside, inhaling the myriad of aromas.

"Be right with you, dear," the older woman behind the counter called out. "Have a look around."

"Thank you."

Other than the two customers she was ringing up, three women were checking out the diffusers shelf. Melinda worked her way around, picked up three candles, and reached the counter at the same time as the other three.

"Go ahead," she told the very pregnant blonde who had set her purchase on the counter.

"Oh, I'm not done shopping. You can buy yours first." She nodded toward the vanilla-nut candle in Melinda's hand. "That's one of my favorites."

"Even without lighting it, I think it will be one of mine also."

"Hey, Lisa, check out this new scent," the dark-haired woman said from the center table. "Black fig and honey." She took a whiff. "*Mmm*, I like this one."

"You like them all, Skye," Lisa replied, leaving Melinda at the counter to join her friend.

"I do, but I only burn them in my office. Clayton says the house smells girly."

The redhead with them rolled her eyes. "As if he'd tell you no to anything."

Lisa and Skye both chuckled, and Lisa said, "Dakota tells you no just to get a rise out of you."

"True, and I do love sparring with him." The redhead's grin and the sparkle in her blue eyes revealed how much she enjoyed teasing the man Melinda assumed was her husband, since she wore a ring.

Skye snorted. "You forget, we know what you love about him."

Melinda forced herself to tune them out, along with her envy of their obvious close friendship, when the woman behind the counter said, "I'm Anna Lee. Did you find everything you wanted?"

She nodded, smiling. "I did but can only get these for now. I'll likely come back for more, as I burn candles whenever I'm inside."

"I'll be here." Ringing her up, Anna Lee cocked her head. "Are you staying nearby, then?"

She hesitated, wary of giving away too much information. After all, the purpose of staying up in the mountains was to keep Cortez from finding her. "Pretty close. I love your shop, and the variety you offer."

"I have fun trying new fragrances when I'm making them."

Anna told her the total, and she pulled

cash from her purse, grateful she wasn't one to pry. She didn't notice the other girls come up behind her. Her stomach rumbled as she handed Anna Lee her money, and she realized how hungry she was. "Can you recommend a place for lunch?"

"Hattie's Deli, and she has the best brownies."

Melinda turned, seeing the redhead right behind her, her eyes still sparkling, this time with friendliness. "Thanks."

She nodded then said, "But if you want something different, the Watering Hole has the best wild game offerings, like elk and buffalo burgers."

"Don't forget their made-from-scratch garlic fries, Poppy," Anna Lee chimed in. "I go there just for those."

"That all sounds good. I've been eating mostly fish this week." Picking up the bag Anna Lee handed her, she smiled at all of them. "Thank you, again."

"Enjoy your stay," Lisa stated as Melinda went to the door with a touch of longing for company to spend the rest of the day with.

She hadn't counted on feeling alone

around people, figured she better get over it or learn to adjust if she intended to stay off Cortez's radar. It would be nice, though, if there were one person she could trust until he was back in prison, someone to help her through this like the last time, when she'd had Nick Rossi.

Melinda sighed as she parked at the Watering Hole, disgusted with the way her mind continued to gravitate toward that one man. She hadn't realized he'd come to mean something to her during those two months, but what happened after he left the safehouse destroyed whatever fragile emotion had been developing.

Trust no one.

Melinda wouldn't forget those words again.

****

Nick couldn't believe it. He swung his head around as what looked like the same Jeep he'd seen at the riding stables drove out of the Watering Hole parking lot. Cutting his engine, he hopped out and tried to see the woman behind the wheel, the same woman who bore an uncanny resemblance to Melinda Walsh the last time he saw her. Only this time, he caught a good enough look to be 90 percent sure the traumatized witness he'd failed to protect was here, in Mountain Bend or staying somewhere nearby.

He didn't believe in coincidence, but since only his family knew he'd relocated here last year, what else could explain her presence? So, the more pressing question he needed answered was why she was here. She'd spoken of the camping trips she'd taken with her mother, but he recalled her saying they hadn't vacationed together since she graduated from college. A lot could happen and change in eighteen months, and maybe, given her close brush with death, she and her mother figured they needed to make the best of each day they had together.

All of that was reasonable, so why was he still getting the weird vibes that told him something wasn't quite right? He was meeting Shawn, Dakota, and Clayton for lunch but didn't see their vehicles in the lot. Leaning against his truck, he pulled out his phone and sought to quell his unease by calling the one person who would know if he needed to be concerned for Melinda.

"Detective Rossi," Captain Honeycutt answered. "It's been a long time. How the hell are you?"

"I'll be better if you can tell me Melinda Walsh is still safe from Cortez." No use beating around the bush when he needed answers. He went taut when Honeycutt paused way too long before answering.

"How'd you know?" he asked, his tone strained.

Fuck. "I didn't. That's why I'm calling. I just saw her."

"Where?" he demanded. "I haven't been able to reach her since I told her Cortez is out. She left San Diego without a word or trace of where she was going. Even her mother doesn't know."

His blood turned cold, fury whipping through Nick as he gripped his phone. "How the hell did that son of a bitch get out already? We had him cold on drug charges."

"He has the money for a damn good lawyer who convinced a judge our warrant didn't include his residence, where we found the detailed records of sales. Only the office where she witnessed her father's execution."

"In other words, bullshit. The evidence at the office led us to his house, and we couldn't wait for him to destroy what was there. Why did she run instead of you helping her?" As soon as he said that, he knew the answer. Melinda didn't trust anyone at the department. "You haven't found the mole yet, right?"

"Right, but I won't give up. I've assigned eyes on Cortez, but I can't keep a twenty-four seven watch on him for long. Not only is it a drain on manpower, but his attorney is bound to file harassment charges if we keep it up, which I told Ms. Walsh."

Shawn and Clayton pulled in and parked next to him. Nick ended the call, intending to enlist their help in tracking down Melinda's whereabouts. He trusted them, but, like her, he didn't trust anyone at his old precinct, and certainly not with the task of keeping her safe again. That included the captain.

Nick decided it wouldn't hurt for him to do his own digging into some of his fellow cops, even if the thought didn't sit well with him. "Keep me updated, if you would, Captain, on all fronts."

"I will if you'll do the same. Let me know if you hear from her."

"You got it," he returned, having no plans to do so until he was positive the captain wasn't the mole. Besides that, there was the fact Melinda hadn't sought him out instead of running, which was why he intended to seek help from friends he would trust with his life.

"You don't look happy," Shawn said, shutting his cruiser door as Nick returned his phone to his pocket.

"We know it's not female related, since you haven't shown much interest in that direction lately." Clayton's blue eyes lit with humor. Dressed in slacks and a sports jacket, the county prosecutor must have just come from court.

Joining them at the door, he gave them a mock frown. "Why is everyone so interested in my sex life? Don't you have enough on your plates with your wives?"

Clayton clapped him on the back before

entering the bar ahead of him and saying over his shoulder, "Sure, but it's entertaining to razz the single guys."

"Glad I can amuse you, but it's not like that."

Nick welcomed the cool, dim interior of the Watering Hole, the only bar in Mountain Bend. He'd been to Boise several times and found Idaho's capital similar to Wyoming's, his home in Cheyenne. But the much smaller town of Mountain Bend appealed to him now, even with the summer influx of tourists crowding the area. From the limited seating options available to them, it appeared a good number of those tourists were having lunch here today.

Clayton nodded to a vacant booth. "Let's grab that."

As soon as they were seated, Shawn wasted no time picking up where Clayton left off. "What's it like, then?"

Nick would have enjoyed teasing them about their penchant for gossip if he weren't grateful for the opening to enlist their help searching for Melinda. The number of patrons in the bar ensured loud conversations would keep anyone from overhearing him, but he still leaned forward to be heard better. "My last case in Cheyenne protecting a witness went bad, and she left without a word. Recently, I've seen her twice around here. I just got off the phone with my old captain when you arrived, and he informed me the drug dealer she was supposed to testify against for murder got out of his drug sentence on a technicality. I need to find her."

Some of the urgency he was feeling must have shown enough to catch their attention because both men frowned in concern, Shawn's gray eyes turning sharp, his gaze assessing. If he hadn't known he was a cop, that look alone would have clued Nick in.

"I can check with the campsites and rental agencies," he offered. "What's her name?"

"That's just it. When I thought it was her at the riding stables the other day, Tuck Matthews checked his roster and she wasn't listed. I'm betting she's going by another name." Even he heard the frustration in his tone, so Clayton's raised brow didn't surprise him.

"Is this guy that much of a threat still? I would think it would be foolish of him to come after her when I'm assuming the cops are keeping an eye on him," Clayton said.

"Going down for first-degree murder comes with life without parole or the death penalty, a big difference from twenty years for drugs, not to mention the recent push to lighten sentences for all drug offenses." Nick hesitated, not willing to reveal yet the depth of Cortez's anger toward Melinda, wanting to protect her privacy for as long as possible until he knew how she'd coped with that trauma all this time. The deliberate assault on her instead of killing her outright, like they had Mike, proved Cortez wanted her to suffer for the trouble she caused him.

The waitress arrived the same time as Dakota joined them, halting the discussion for now. Sliding in next to Nick, Dakota ordered a beer along with the rest of them, and she left saying she'd be right back to take their orders. Shawn wasted no time filling him in, Dakota's black gaze swinging toward Nick when the sheriff finished.

"What can we do to help?"

Nick's tension went down a notch, gratitude filling him from their quick, unquestioning support. Being the new guy around town and in the club, he hadn't expected such unwavering acceptance of both himself and a botched op he hadn't yet fully explained.

"Odds are her presence in this area, so close to me, is a coincidence since I only told my family my relocation plans. If I can find her and convince her I'm not the cop in the department who betrayed her, I can keep her safe from this guy until he's back in prison. I have no doubt she'll still refuse to testify against him until my old precinct spits out the traitor." Their expressions mirrored his anger and disgust with the person who would not only betray their oath to serve and protect but would deliberately put an innocent person in harm's way for money.

While they ate, they asked him several questions regarding Cortez, the case against him, and what he knew about Melinda. Nick had once believed he knew her well, after all the time they'd spent together in the safehouse, but there were gaps he couldn't answer. Her mother and aunt were the only relatives she mentioned, but he didn't know her aunt's married name. She worked as a hospice nurse and mentioned a few friends in passing. They'd spent more time discussing movies than details about each other's lives.

"That's little to go on but not impossible," Shawn stated, pushing his empty plate away. "I can start by contacting campsites and cabin rentals and asking for names of cash-paying customers. Without a warrant, it'll be up to them on how much info I can get." He looked toward Clayton who shrugged.

"I can try to get you one and hope for a sympathetic judge. Since she's unwilling to testify, it's doubtful unless you ask your former captain for a material witness warrant. That's likely your best bet."

"I won't do that to her, not after what she went through." Nick would not betray Melinda by letting anyone force her into testifying.

"You're sure it's her you saw?" Dakota asked after finishing off his brew.

"Not the first time at the stables. I was too far away. Today, I got a close enough look when she drove right by me leaving this parking lot to confirm my suspicions." And he'd been itching to move on finding her ever since.

The waitress returned with their checks and, as they each paid, Shawn said, "Give me a few days to see where I get on my end then we'll go from there. We haven't let any of our girls down so far, and we won't start with yours."

Nick shook his head, not wanting them to go into this with the wrong impression. "She's not..."

Clayton laughed as they slid out of the booth then clapped him on the back. "That's what we all said in the beginning, Rossi. Don't bother wasting your energy or breath on denials."

Along with Shawn, even stern-faced Dakota showed his amusement when his lips quirked at that. He didn't bother setting them straight as he owed them for their help. Allowing them some fun at his expense was a small price to pay for their support.

"I'll be in touch," Shawn told him as they walked out and dispersed to their separate vehicles.

Nick paused with his hand on the door handle, looking over the hood at the three of them. "Thanks, all of you. I appreciate it."

Dakota cocked his head, his dark eyes hidden behind the lowered brim of his Stetson. "Was it that bad, your botched op?"

It didn't surprise Nick that Dakota had assessed his face and mood with such accuracy. All the Doms he'd met since exploring the lifestyle seemed to possess an aptitude for reading people.

Nodding, he replied, "Worse." Leaving them with a wave, he returned to the ranch, hoping work would keep him from chomping at the bit waiting to hear back from Shawn.

****

"What do you have for me?" Cortez demanded as soon as his contact answered the phone. Thankfully, he'd used a burner phone in his dealings with this person, and others, and the first thing he'd done upon his release was to dig out his extras from the basement.

"Nothing, same as the last time you called, and the same as I'll have if you call again. I don't owe you anything else and, as I said, I'm done."

Gritting his teeth, Cortez worked to get himself under control. It wouldn't do to alienate his only cop source just yet. If he had any other option, he would have found a way to off the bastard as soon as he was released. Instead, he was stuck until he could get hold of his hacker and get his results. With luck, his lawyer would have the goons taken off his ass by then.

"You're done when I say you are," he snapped, injecting as much threat into his voice as he could. "You've got contacts – use them."

"No one is talking, and I mean no one. I can't even find out if the captain has talked her into returning to testify. Look, I came through for you last time, and nothing has changed. I still don't know how they found your men at that warehouse; I just know it wasn't through me. If I ask too many questions, suspicion will fall on me, and that's a risk I'm not willing to take."

"You'd rather risk being dead?" Cortez almost laughed at his informant's indrawn breath, but the reply he got wiped away his humor.

"You know, Cortez, the only thing stopping Ms. Walsh from testifying is her distrust of the cops until the mole is caught. If I turn myself in, you'll be the one facing a death penalty, or, at the very least, a life sentence. Remember that."

Not if she's dead, along with you.

Looking out his front window at the obvious cop car, Cortez gripped the phone, his fury white-hot. He regretted the day Theo had gotten the balls to copy records with the intention of turning him in to the cops. He might have been considered small-time among drug barons, but he'd made a cushy life for himself, with enough to keep six thugs on his payroll and an accountant too scared of him to do anything except his job.

Now, here he was, forced to pay his sleazy lawyer extra to access his hidden accounts to stay afloat, his henchmen all dead, his cop ally bailing on him, and his revenge against Theo witnessed by the guy's daughter. Of all the fucking luck.

"You should remember what I do to people who betray me. Where there's a will, there's a way. Get me something, or you'll find out firsthand the strength of my will." He hung up and looked up an old contact he hadn't used in a long time due to the high cost of doing business with him. Given his limited options, which included his source's reluctance to help him again, he was left with no other choices. "Barry, Anthony Cortez," he stated as soon as Barry answered. "I need a few people found. You interested?"

Cortez hung up ten minutes later, his temper threatening to boil over. Barry hadn't changed and still drove a hard, expensive bargain, but he was good at hacking to find people, even those who didn't want to be located. He spent the rest of the evening drinking and contemplating revenge against everyone who was intent on betraying him. It had been easy to keep track of the two surviving detectives from his men's raid on that safehouse until last year when Rossi had quit the force and moved away. Unless the Walsh bitch changed her mind and agreed once again to testify against him, his lawyer couldn't insist on Rossi's return. Detective Philips retired early and had gone on disability following his injuries, his retirement a matter of public notice, and Cortez's lawyer confirmed he still resided in Cheyenne. Once Barry came through with Ms. Walsh's and Detective Rossi's locations, he would call in a few favors and enlist help in getting to their locations without the cops finding out. He'd have to wait until Honeycutt was ordered to pull the tail on him, but after that, he would waste no time in getting even.

Just imagining what he would do to them improved his mood.

****

Nick rode into the stable yard astride a white mare named Baby, pleased with the way she'd performed riding the herd and her easy disposition. Her buyers wanted the horse for both ranch work and for their ten-year-old daughter to ride, and he was now confident Baby would make a good match for the family. Focusing on work these past two days had kept him from obsessing over Melinda's whereabouts and safety during the day. But at night, when he returned to the house alone, she was all he could think about.

Chastising himself for acting like an idiot didn't help, neither did questioning why he should worry so much. She was a grown woman who had made her choices, choices he should respect by leaving her alone. From the little he could put together, she'd taken smart precautions since learning of Cortez's release, and, if she needed anything, Captain Honeycutt was a phone call away from sending her help.

Dismounting, Nick thought he should let it go. He was no longer a cop for several reasons, one the opportunity to return to his roots and ranch life, both of which he loved. He ran a hand down the mare's neck, her sleek muscles quivering under his palm. There was nothing quite like having fifteen-hundred pounds of solid muscle taking you across a wide-open range with hooves pounding into the earth. The only thing better was bringing a woman to a much-needed orgasm and feeling her slick muscles grip his fingers or cock.

Like when he'd brought Melinda to climax.

"Shit." So much for letting her situation, and her, go.

"I thought she did good, boss," Jose said, joining him at the rail.

Loosening the saddle strap, Nick flashed his hired hand a rueful grin. "She did great. I was mumbling about something else." He removed the saddle and hefted it onto his shoulder. "After you clean her up for the new owners who are coming in the morning, you and Spencer can call it a day."

Jose's dark, perspiration-streaked face broke out into a wide smile. "That will make my girl happy."

"Glad I can oblige your love life. See you in the morning."

Nick returned the saddle to the stable then strode to the house, his phone pealing as he entered. Seeing Shawn's name, he went taut with expectation, those pesky prickles racing across his skin telling him this was important.

"Hey, did you find out something?"

"Yes, and it wasn't difficult since people around here know and trust me. Pine Tree cabin rentals has a cash-paying customer named Linda Greer. Greer is Cara Walsh's sister's married name. It could be coincidence but worth checking out. When do you want to go?"

If it was Melinda, she wouldn't welcome him showing up out of the blue, let alone another cop. "If you don't mind, I'll have better luck with her if I go alone."

Doubt crept into Shawn's voice as he asked, "Are you sure? You said she doesn't trust anyone connected to the case, which I'm not. Sounds like I'd have a better shot with her."

Nick wasn't thinking straight or he would have thought of that. Why would he fare better alone when he must be at the top of her list of people she no longer trusted? "You're right. Why do I get the feeling I'm going into an uphill battle?"

"You tell me. I'll come by your place around seven. It's a thirty-minute drive once we reach the rental office."

"Thanks, Shawn. See you in the morning." Nick tossed his phone on the kitchen counter, hoping he got a decent night's sleep tonight. He would need his wits about him for seeing Melinda again.

Chapter Four

Birds fluttered through the trees as Melinda followed the trail from the stream back to her cabin. Carrying her catches, two rainbow trout and one bull, she looked forward to dinner. It was these moments, however, when she missed her mother, the companionship and fun they used to have camping together. More than once since coming here, she'd asked herself why they'd stopped taking those annual trips. Once she graduated from nursing school, there'd been time, and now she regretted they'd let those vacations lapse.

She'd gotten so used to the silence beyond nature's echoes from the surrounding woods that she found herself taken aback when the rumble of an engine reached her just before she emerged at the cabin. Pausing in the clearing, she debated whether to stay out of sight in the forest or dash inside, then did neither, thinking Cortez wouldn't blatantly come up to her door. No, he would either send another goon after her or creep up on her and take her by surprise. After his henchmen gleefully told her he'd ordered her tortured before being killed, she'd never doubted he would make her pay tenfold for the time and money she'd cost him if given the chance.

Melinda breathed a sigh of relief when she saw a local police cruiser roll to a stop next to her Jeep then went rigid in shock as Nick Rossi slid out of the passenger side. *No way. My luck can't be this bad.* What was he doing here? How had he found her? A million other questions went through her head, eying his familiar tall body, broad shoulders, and shadowed jawline below his Stetson. Memories assailed her, good and bad, the foremost his hard hold and experienced hands bringing her to an exalted plane of pleasure she'd never been able to forget. She went hot then cold as the glint from the sun hitting the badge on the man who stood behind the open driver's side door caught her attention.

He tipped his hat but stayed where he was to introduce himself. "Ma'am. I'm Sheriff McDuff. From your expression just now, I'm assuming you remember Nick Rossi."

Struggling to swallow past the lump lodged in her throat, she kept her gaze on the sheriff. "What can I do for you, Sheriff?"

To her annoyance, he let Nick speak instead of answering. "Melinda, we need to talk. Honeycutt told me Cortez is out."

The familiarity of his rough, deep voice washed through Melinda, warming her insides, threatening her composure. She tried to remain focused on the here and now, instead of drifting back to those days when she trusted him with her life. He still looked damn good in jeans and boots, his dark hair curling around his nape, his hat tipped low. He'd traded the sport coats and dress shirts he'd worn in Cheyenne for a work shirt with the first three buttons left open to reveal a sprinkle of dark, curling chest hair. It didn't matter what persona he portrayed, though, she couldn't let her guard down around him again.

"We don't need to do anything, Detective. I'm not going to testify, so you and I are still done." She dragged her gaze away from his tight, disapproving expression and looked at the sheriff. "If there's nothing else, I have fish to clean."

Sheriff McDuff was every bit as sexy and good-looking as Nick but that didn't seem to matter to her traitorous body and heart. Both were still clamoring for Nick, even after all this time, and without ruling out the possibility he was the one who sold her out.

"Ms. Walsh, if I can find you, so can others. I would trust Nick Rossi with my life, and I wouldn't have brought him here if I didn't think it was in your best interest. Talk to him. I'll drive around the bend but stay within calling distance."

The sheriff slid behind the wheel as Nick shut his door, and Melinda's mouth went dry when he sauntered toward her. She didn't fear him, or being alone with him. Maybe that made her a fool, but it was her susceptibility to his nearness she worried about more than anything. Her strong reaction to seeing him again didn't bode well for dealing with him, or keeping her distance.

Straightening her backbone, she held her ground as he stopped in front of her and she breathed in his earthy scent. "You've come a long way for nothing, Detective. I'm not going back into protective custody, and I'm not testifying unless the traitor in your department is found."

She gave him brownie points for not flinching when his eyes went to her scars, and herself a pat on the back for maintaining her composure when his enticing lips curled up at the corners.

"Not so far, Melinda. I own a ranch just outside of Mountain Bend where I've lived the last year. And it's no longer my department." He cocked his head, that small smile disappearing. "I know Captain Honeycutt told you I quit."

He *lived* here? How could she be so unlucky? If she believed in kismet, she would think this chance meeting was meant to be, that a force beyond her comprehension or control had a hand in her choosing this area to hide out. But she didn't believe in fate, so she put it down to plain bad luck.

"He told me a lot of things, like I could trust the cops to keep me safe." Moving around him, she walked over to the rough wood plank attached to the side of the cabin and plunked down the fish. Reaching for the large knife sitting on top, she started cleaning and deboning, hoping he got the hint and went away.

He didn't. Nick's large, warm hand landed on her shoulder, and, even wearing a T-shirt, his grip brought back the comfort of his firm hold the last time they were this close.

"It wasn't me, Melinda. You have to know that."

"No, I don't." She brought the knife down with extra force, removing the bull trout's head. He sighed, and his breath tickled the back of her neck, raising goose bumps along her arms.

"Will you at least put that down, turn around, and talk to me?"

It was the hint of exasperation in his tone that prompted her to do as he asked, pleased she could get to him on some level, the same as he with her.

"What is it you want from me, Nick? Like you said, you're not in law enforcement anymore, and it's no longer your case. So, why are you here, and, for that matter, how did you find me?" She'd thought she'd done a good job hiding her trail, but what were the odds she'd come across Nick while trying to keep Cortez from finding her?

Lifting his hat, he raked his fingers through his hair then put it back on and fisted his hands on his hips. She didn't need to see under the lowered brim to know his dark-brown gaze remained pinned on her.

"To finish what I started eighteen months ago, ensure your safety." Concern slid past the frustration coloring his tone as he said, "I saw you the other day in Mountain Bend, contacted Honeycutt, and found out about Cortez getting released, and I was worried about you. You'd be safer in town, or staying at my place."

She was shaking her head before he finished. "I'm fine right here. I have my hunting rifle and phone, and Captain

Honeycutt will let me know if he's forced to remove the tag he has on Cortez. You can return to your ranch with a clear conscience."

"I don't remember you being this stubborn," he stated with a quizzical tilt of his head, as if he didn't know what to make of a side of her he'd never seen before.

Without thinking, she lifted a hand to her face and fingered the scar on her cheek. The blemish was as smooth as the rest of her skin, the line so pale it was hardly noticeable, but she could find it in her sleep if need be. "Getting carved up while the assailants laughed changes a person. Not to mention witnessing yet another point-blank, murderous shooting." Dropping her arm, she tightened with remorse over the pain etched on his face. "I never got the chance to tell you I'm sorry about Mike. If it hadn't been for me..."

He held up his hand and issued a hard command. "Stop. His death isn't your fault any more than it's mine. Cortez will pay for Mike, as well as for your dad, someday. I may not be a cop anymore, but your case will stay mine until I get vindication for both Mike and you."

Nick had possessed the same passionate stance against injustice when they'd first met. The difference now was, could she believe the emotion behind his vow was real? When memories of those weeks would consume her, she would separate her thoughts into before and after that last night in the safehouse. Before, Melinda would never have doubted his commitment to his job. Since then, all she'd done was question it, and him.

"You'll do what you have to, and so will I." Pointing toward the bend in the narrow road leading to the cabin and where she could see the sheriff's taillights, she said, "Your friend is waiting for you."

Nick's jaw went rigid, his displeasure obvious. "Will you at least think about accepting my help?"

No. She gave him a soft smile and lied. "Sure."

Shaking his head, he pivoted and strode several feet away before tossing over his shoulder, "I'll be back."

Melinda replied without thought, her response automatic. "*The Terminator*, 1984,

Arnold Schwarzenegger." She realized her blunder as soon as the words slipped out and he spun around, the surprise and pleasure on his face impossible to miss.

A slow grin creased Nick's cheeks, and he tipped his hat. "See you soon, darlin'."

He left her irritated with herself, befuddled over her conflicting emotions, and struggling with how to deal with him when he returned. And what was with calling her darlin' in that slow, sexy drawl that curled her toes and made her pussy clench in need? Melinda didn't know whether to fantasize about throttling him or look forward to his return.

****

Nick's hopes of breaking through the shield Melinda had erected between them surged after hearing her quick, unthinking comeback when he said he would return. He had issued the statement literally, not as a movie quote. Her answer proved her mind had been on their past bond and their shared interest in movies rather than on believing he had betrayed her. She was the first person he'd met who shared his obsession with movie trivia, and if he could continue reminding her of those weeks when she'd given him her unwavering trust, he stood a chance at keeping her safer this time around.

"Let's go," Nick told Shawn as soon as he got into the cruiser.

Shifting into gear, he asked, "No luck with her?"

"Not today, but I won't give up trying."

Seeing the woman who had preyed on his conscience for so long resurrected the strong feelings he once felt for Melinda. Those intense emotions were wrong then, and wrong now as they distracted from the big issue – keeping her safe from a drug dealer's retribution. But he'd be damned if he didn't find himself as hard-pressed with lust and want for Melinda today as he was the night he'd left her with his fingers coated with her cream and her soft cries of release ringing in his ears.

"She's stunning, even with the faint scars. Gotta admire how she doesn't try to hide them or avert her face away from others. Souvenirs of your botched protection detail?"

Nick grabbed the side handle as they bounced over the uneven terrain, agreeing with Shawn. Melinda hadn't looked away from him once, not even when he'd shifted toe to toe with her, close enough to make out each white line and see himself reflected in the vivid blue of her eyes. He had admired the hell out of her willingness to testify against someone like Cortez, the way she'd vowed to see her father's killer paid for his crime. His high regard for her had gone up a notch today when she held her face up without flinching.

"The bastards were ordered to torture her in front of my partner before killing them. We arrived in time to save her life but not his. We didn't have anything to connect the dead assailants to Cortez, which didn't help our case."

"As much as I sympathize with your feelings about the case, Nick, my hands are tied regarding Ms. Walsh. I can't force her into accepting protection, nor do I have the manpower to keep sending someone to check on her." Shawn pulled to a stop in front of

Nick's house and turned to face him. "What are your plans, if you don't mind me asking?"

"Camp on her doorstep if that's my only option. I won't let him hurt her again, not if I can help it this time. Cortez is a mean bastard, and I've no doubt he has hidden accounts we didn't find, enough money to hire more druggies to do his bidding. I wouldn't put it past him to want to come after her himself."

"He's still got a watch on him, though, doesn't he?" Shawn asked.

"Yes, and that helps. I trust my captain to let me know if that changes. The same as you, he doesn't have the manpower or budget to keep it up for long. Once I convince Melinda she can trust me as much now as she did before someone betrayed her, she can stay with me."

"From the little I witnessed, that won't be easy," Shawn returned, his tone dry, his face reflecting sympathy.

"Nothing worthwhile ever is, but she deserves the effort. Thanks. I appreciate your time today." Nick opened the door and slid out, glancing back when Shawn spoke again.

"You need anything, let me know. If it's

in my power, I'll help."

Nodding, Nick shut the door and entered his house, grateful for such loyal friendship. He still grieved Mike's death, and missed his friend and partner. The loss of that close relationship and guilt over Melinda's ordeal kept him from forming attachments when he moved here. Funny, he mused now, he'd never noticed when others were sliding their way past his defenses.

Maybe he would get lucky again in dealing with Melinda's reticence.

The next morning, Nick decided persistence was the key to gaining Melinda's trust. He helped with the chores and then went to Merry's stall where the distrustful mare greeted him with a snap of her large teeth.

"Is that any way to treat the hand that feeds you?" The damaged mare tossed her head and pawed the ground in an apparent bitchy mood. "So you're going to be like that today, huh? Okay, have it your way." He pivoted and took three steps before she whinnied in complaint. More than she disliked people and horses alike, Merry detested confinement.

Returning to her stall, he again reached out a hand and she again went for him, and he started to leave. It took another two attempts at bait and switch before she backed up a step instead of trying to bite him. "At least you're not aiming to eat my hand for a snack now." He entered the stall and clipped the lead onto her bridle. When she left the stable without kicking up a fuss, he figured the time was well spent this morning. Merry's hooves would need tending soon, and he didn't want to risk her taking a chunk out of his hide, literally, when he did the chore.

Nick snatched an apple from a barrel at the stable door and turned her loose in the pasture before tossing it to her. Spenser strolled up, and Nick sent him an amused look. "Not even a thank you from her."

Spenser chuckled. "I say count yourself lucky she didn't break a bone with a kick or take a chunk out of you with those teeth."

"She's coming around. Slow, but getting there."

Squinting his blue eyes, Spenser eyed the mare chomping on the apple, her wary gaze glued to them, her tail swishing. "Yeah, she is. You've done good, boss. We're heading out to check the fence line if you don't need anything else right now."

"Go ahead. I'll be gone for most of the afternoon but should get back before you two leave. If not, I'll see you in the morning."

"Have a good one."

Nick waited while Spenser and Jose mounted and rode out, thinking how he'd lucked out hiring them from Dakota's referral. He took a sweeping gaze of his land, the horses he enjoyed training to work for others, the small herd he hoped brought in a little extra income, and the house he was slowly making his own. Seeing Melinda again, the fear she couldn't hide even though she tried, the determination to do things her way this time around, had erased the content he'd found here. He needed that sense of gratification back as much as he needed to salve his conscience by ensuring she stayed safe.

Checking the time, he saw he could get into Mountain Bend, pick up lunch, and be at her cabin right around noon. He remembered her healthy appetite and how he, Mike, and Owen would tease her about where she put all the calories. She could outeat each of them and not gain an ounce but seemed to have lost weight when he saw her yesterday. With luck, the order he called into the Watering Hole earlier would earn him some favorable points.

Nick parked in front of Melinda's cabin an hour later, his blood running cold as he got out and heard gunshots coming from the woods. Grabbing his rifle, he followed the firing echoes, swearing if she was harmed, he wouldn't hesitate to take out whoever had caused her injury. Later, he would beat himself up over not insisting she come back with him yesterday. Three shots rang out followed by a deafening, nerve-racking silence that turned his gut into a ball of nausea.

Coming to a clearing, he stopped and drew a deep breath of relief, taking a moment to get himself and his jangled nerves under control before letting Melinda know he was here. A rifle leaned against a log, and she stood with her hands on her slim hips, staring down at the three cans lined up on another log, none of them touched by bullets. Her huff of annoyance made him smile and eased the last of his taut muscles. A stirring of lust warmed his cold blood as he eyed her slender legs in denim cutoffs that hugged her heart-shaped ass. Her hair was pulled back in a braid just like yesterday, and he itched to loosen the tie and fist his hand in the long, silky strands. He would welcome the return of his interest in sex if those stirrings weren't for a woman who wanted nothing to do with him.

Her shoulders tensed right before she whirled around, reaching for her rifle. Seeing him, the look on her face went from alarmed to annoyed in a heartbeat. She picked up her gun, scowling, showing no sign of fear or even wariness at finding herself alone in the woods with a man she supposedly didn't trust. He realized the significance of that but doubted she did, or would welcome him pointing it out to her.

"If I'd been holding my rifle, I might have shot you for sneaking up on me," she retorted, coming toward him.

"Really?" He cocked his head toward the untouched cans. "Somehow, I doubt that."

"You're a lot bigger target than the cans, and I'm out of practice. I haven't picked up a gun in ten years. Why are you here?"

She halted a foot away from him, her blue eyes steady on his face. He'd give anything to see them brighten with pleasure like before whenever he entered the safehouse, or darken with arousal like when he'd caved and put his hands on her, his fingers in her.

"I brought lunch." When she started to shake her head, he said, "Pulled pork sandwiches, coleslaw, and mini chocolate lava cakes." As he'd hoped, sweets were still her weakness, judging by the way her expression switched from *no way* to *yes please*.

Her slim brows dipped in a frown. "I suppose the price is you staying to eat with me."

"You suppose correctly." Taking her elbow, he steered her back toward the cabin. "Hearing those shots when I arrived took ten years off my life. The least you can do is enjoy a meal with me."

"Since you arrived uninvited, don't expect me to feel bad. Like I said, I can take care of myself." Melinda lifted her hand holding the rifle and pulled out of his light clasp. Reaching her cabin, she seemed to realize he'd come by himself this time.

The flash of uncertainty in her eyes cut him to the quick, but Nick told himself there was good reason for her leeriness. "Relax, Melinda. If I'd been on the take with Cortez, I could have taken you out anytime during those two months waiting for trial or in the last year and a half."

"If you'd acted too soon in Cheyenne, suspicion would have fallen on you three. And there was no reason to risk prison by coming after me in San Diego after I refused to testify and he was already serving time."

There were still holes in her logic, but he refrained from pointing them out. She wouldn't listen or let herself trust him again until she was ready. Ignoring her, he retrieved lunch from his truck and strolled past her to the picnic table. "I'm hungry. Are you joining me?" He removed his Stetson and sat down with his back to her but could picture her standing there in indecision and didn't breathe easy until she huffed and joined him. Those minor temper fits amused him as much now as the rare displays before, those mostly during their heated card games.

Melinda slid onto the bench across the redwood table from Nick, and he handed her a sandwich. Opening the wrapper, she said, "I'm still not leaving the cabin."

"I figured. Will you let me give you a few shooting pointers before I leave?"

"Not necessary. I just need practice. It'll come back to me. In the meantime, I can fish and brought plenty of food with me." She bit into the thick sandwich with relish, and barbeque sauce dripped down her chin.

Nick resisted the urge to lean over and lick it off and press his mouth against her stubborn lips. Too bad she wasn't one of the submissives at Spurs. Then he could just order her to comply with his wishes for her safety.

"You mentioned camping with your mom a lot when you were younger. Why did you quit going?" He took a swig of bottled water while she swallowed before answering.

"After college, I started working long hours, taking some private duty nursing jobs. Those were hard to schedule vacations around. Before we knew it, we'd gotten away from taking those trips together."

"I can tell you miss them. Does she know you're here?"

She gave him a narrow-eyed glare. "Trying to find out who I'm in touch with while here?"

Anger rose to the surface, and he returned her glare. "I could have done away with you several times by now and hid your body where no one would find it for months, if at all, *if* that's why I'm here."

She paused with a plastic forkful of coleslaw halfway to her mouth, her expression turning thoughtful. Taking the bite, she waited to speak without food in her mouth, his humor returning at her politeness.

"You expect me to believe you want to pick up where you left off in Cheyenne in protecting me? After all this time and when you're no longer a cop? Why should I believe that?"

"Because I was there for you for two

months. That has to have earned some trust from you," he shot back.

He jolted when her eyes grew watery, and she whispered with an ache in her voice, "But you weren't there when I needed you most, were you, Detective Rossi? And I still wonder why that is, why Cortez's men waited until that night, right before I was set to testify, when you weren't there, to attack." Her face paled, and she scrubbed a hand over her eyes. *"Crap."*

Her words hit him like a sucker punch to the gut. "I don't have an answer for that." He wished to God he did because he'd wondered the same thing and had spent months searching for the answers to no avail. "Here." Handing her the bag still holding the chocolate lava servings, he pushed to his feet. "I'll leave the desserts with you. I have to get going. Keep your rifle with you at all times."

Nick forced himself to walk away without looking back, hoping he didn't regret leaving her here alone for now.

Chapter Five

Melinda sat at the table and waited until Nick drove off before delving into the bag for dessert, ignoring the leaden ball of guilt cramping her abdomen. Seeing him again had resurrected feelings, insecurities, and questions she preferred remained buried and unanswered. From the moment she'd first met Detective Rossi, he'd turned her inside out with the deep timbre of his voice and his potent, dark-eyed gaze. For two months, he'd made her not only the focus of his protection but his undivided attention. She hadn't realized how much that meant to her, how much *he* meant to her until betrayal had upended her life.

The pain, terror, and breach of trust on that final night had obliterated the positive aspects of those weeks. The other two detectives were nice but never went the lengths to befriend her that Nick had, never took time to get to know her or showed an interest in her other than as a job. Nick had gone above and beyond his job requirement of keeping her safe. She thought he liked her for her, enjoyed her company, and was growing to want her as much as she craved him. She'd been on the cusp of falling in love when everything had fallen apart. Afterward, her days and nights were consumed with physical and emotional pain.

She'd returned home wanting nothing more than to get back to her life and forget how trying to do the right thing had ended up going so wrong. It had taken weeks of recovery for her wounds to heal enough for plastic surgery and months before the knife slices started to fade. The whispers, looks, struggle to regain control of her life had taken a toll on her. She thought she'd managed quite well with her mother and aunt's support and love – that was until she set eyes on Nick again and those stirrings picked up the moment she saw him. She realized she'd deluded herself all that time into believing she'd gotten over him and couldn't afford a repeat of those deeper emotions.

"Not going there again," she muttered, delving into the bag he'd left on the table. Opening the Styrofoam box, she almost drooled at the chocolate cake he'd hinted was filled with soft fudge. Sweets, especially decadent desserts, were her weakness, and, considering her volatile reaction to Nick after all this time, she worried he just might be another one.

Melinda saved the second piece for later and went back to target practice, determined to take out the three cans this time. She'd mistakenly thought she would still be a decent shot even though a decade had passed since she'd last picked up a rifle. Bracing her feet apart, she lifted the gun, took aim, and fired, this time hitting the end can well enough to topple it from the log. When she turned in later that night, her arms were sore, but her aim had improved. Her mind was a different matter though, still awash with conflicting questions and doubts about Nick. With luck, he'd gotten the message she didn't trust him or the circumstances regarding her botched protection detail and wouldn't keep bothering her.

Late afternoon the next day, she returned to the cabin from hiking and fishing looking forward to a shower and glass of wine with dinner only to find Nick's four-door, bright-orange Ford Ranger parked near the edge of the woods. Cursing his tenaciousness, she tossed her catch on the cleaning plank and followed whistling coming from one of the narrow trails into the trees. Several yards into the dense forest, she found him pitching a small tent on the mossy ground. He glanced up at her from where he was crouched down, hammering a spike into the earth.

His nudged his hat up, hitting her with a megawatt grin that revealed the lines around his eyes and dimple in his left cheek. "Hello, darlin'. I can help you clean those fish in a minute."

Melinda bristled at his nonchalant attitude and her quick-fire response to his heated look as he didn't bother hiding his appreciation of her bare legs in shorts. "I don't need your help and don't want you here."

"*Mmmm*, I think I've heard that before." He returned his attention to securing his tent, asking, "Didn't your mother ever tell you you don't always get what you want?"

"Damn it, Nick." She resisted the urge to stomp her foot in frustration. "You can't camp here. I rented this property for the next month."

"And I talked John Ingram at Pine Tree Rentals into letting me stay here, so you can quit wasting your breath with that argument."

Pushing to his feet, she could see his quad muscles bunch under his jeans and recalled the bulge of those muscles pressed against her legs when he'd pinned her against the bedroom wall that night. Why did she retain such vivid memories of a man she swore she couldn't risk putting her faith in again? That was just one of several questions she tabled for later, when she wasn't grubby, hungry, and out of sorts.

"Fine, just don't bother me."

Spinning around, she stomped back to the cabin and took her frustration out on the dead fish, preparing them for the pan in record time. In the kitchen, she diced the skinned, deboned trout and mixed it with rice, spinach, and cheese before sliding it into the oven and going to take a much-needed shower. Standing under the lukewarm spray, another memory pushed past her efforts to forget about Nick's nearness.

Melinda walked out of the bathroom wrapped in a towel, shivering against the cool air-conditioned air, halting in surprise at seeing Detective Rossi enter her room. "What's happened?" she asked, his frantic expression alarming her.

Nick seemed to release a breath, his broad shoulders relaxing when he whipped his head toward her. "Sorry. You didn't answer my knock."

His eyes raked her damp body, and her nipples puckered in response, her pussy spasming with an aching need she'd lived with now for five weeks. A warm flush stole over her face, yet she couldn't look away from the blatant appreciation and lust swirling his gaze. She did the only thing she could come up with considering the awkwardness of the moment.

"Well, nobody's perfect."

His eyes lit with appreciation and humor. "Good one, Melinda. Some Like It Hot, 1959, Monroe, Curtis, and Lemmon. Owen's here with dinner."

Nick had walked out, leaving her standing there craving him with every cell in her body. Melinda never imagined she would find herself in the same needy state a year and a half later despite having every reason to keep her distance this time around.

She dressed in loose gym shorts and a Padres T-shirt and ate dinner in lonely silence. Disgusted with her wishy-washy mood swings involving Nick, she scooped some of the casserole onto a paper plate and took it out to him, getting a little satisfaction from his startled surprise when he saw her.

"I made enough for ten people," she said, thrusting the plate toward him when he walked over to greet her.

"Thank you, darlin'."

He reached for the plate and their fingers brushed, the unexpected spark from that light contact startling her into yanking her hand back as if burned. "Quit calling me that," she snapped, uncomfortable with the warm glow his endearment generated each time he dragged out the word in a deep rumble.

Ignoring her outburst, he held up the plate. "Looks good, and I haven't gotten around to eating yet. Will you join me?"

"No, I ate. Good night."

Melinda returned to the cabin, locked up, and spent the evening wondering what he was up to and a sleepless night dreaming of that large, strong body pinning her to the bed. She awoke listening to birds singing outside her window and the aroma of coffee tickling her nose. As soon as the cobwebs of sleep cleared from her head, she frowned and jumped out of bed, realizing her coffee maker didn't have a timer.

"Now you're breaking and entering?" she accused Nick, finding him in the kitchen pouring coffee into a travel mug.

"Nonsense. That's illegal. Just a small exercise proving how fallible you are here." Facing her, he snapped a lid on the mug, his mouth curling in a taunting grin. "And would you look at this. I was here all night and managed not to harm you in any way." He walked by her, nodding to the mug. "Thanks. I didn't want to take time to brew my own. See you this evening."

Ignoring the logic of his cryptic remark, she asked, "Don't you have to work?"

"Yes," he tossed back, opening the door, "but some things are more important."

Melinda either stayed clear of Nick or ignored him if they came within talking distance of each other over the next several days but admitted she slept better knowing she wasn't alone in the woods. That wasn't enough to change her mind about giving him the same level of trust as when he guarded her in Cheyenne, so she spent the fifth day in Mountain Bend and the night at Miner's Junction B&B. As much as she relished the softer bed, hotter water, and historic ambiance of the renovated 1880s stately home, she preferred the rustic cabin. Jen, the proprietress expecting her first baby, joined her for the breakfast buffet and filled her in on the town's history and residents.

She left the B&B feeling smug about

thwarting Nick until that evening when he returned showing no signs her absence the night before bothered him. He parked in the same spot, and she flushed under his direct, potent look unobstructed by his Stetson. "You would do us both a favor if you would stay at the B&B every night."

Surprised, she stuttered, "How'd you..."

"It's a small town, darlin', even during tourist season. Speaking of which, I'm hosting a picnic this Sunday. I hope you'll come."

With a wave, he disappeared into the woods, whistling. Melinda's first thought was whether the women she'd met the day she'd visited town or Jen would attend the picnic. Then she couldn't figure out whether to laugh or stomp her foot in annoyance at how he'd derailed her petty revenge with his announcement.

****

"Found them."

Cortez wallowed in satisfaction at hearing Barry's announcement. Confident the burner phone wouldn't leave a record or the phone be traced, he asked, "Where?"

"Funny thing, they're both right next door. Idaho," Barry answered with a hint of amusement.

"You're kidding. Walsh and Rossi? Are they together?" He couldn't believe his luck in finding the detective in charge of his case and Rossi's eye witness within driving distance. His police contact had sworn not to know Rossi's whereabouts following his departure from the force, but now Cortez found that hard to believe.

"It doesn't appear that way in print. She's renting a mountain cabin, and he owns a small spread about forty miles from where she's staying."

"What's she doing there?" He'd never met the woman or even seen her face. When he sent his men to check out a sound from the office seconds after he'd blown Theo away, they had only caught sight of her disappearing taillights. Through his lawyer, he'd learned who she was, where she was from, and what she would say on the stand.

"Don't know. You just hired me to get

her location. She rented the place using her aunt's married name, which was easy enough to discover once I dug up everyone tied to her in any way, shape, or form."

"Excellent." Barry was the best computer hacker around. His talent and the fact he'd never been caught had always amazed Cortez, even if he didn't like the guy. Glaring at the ever-present cop car out front, he said, "I have one more thing for you to do for me."

"It'll cost you."

"It'll cost you more if you screw it up. I'll call you back in twenty-four hours or less." Cortez hung up, making plans in his head to end Melinda Walsh's hold over his future once and for all. But she wasn't the only one who would pay the price for daring to take a stand against him. The two surviving detectives would also suffer before he slipped into Canada to start a new life. Philips was a cripple, still living in Cheyenne, and would be easy to eliminate. Rossi and the girl would require more thought.

****

A summer storm rolled in two nights later, opening up a deluge with accompanying high winds shortly after midnight. Nick had left Spurs early to beat the forecasted weather but hadn't counted on the ferocity of a superstorm. He slipped his rain slicker over his head, picked up his rifle, and left the flimsy tent before it came down around him, cursing as the cold rain blew into his face. He slid his thumb to the switch on his flashlight then paused when he noticed a flicker of light bouncing around in the trees.

"Fuck," he swore, assuming the worst.

The inclement weather all but guaranteed to keep other nearby campers inside, which meant whoever was sneaking around the woods this late, in this weather, was up to no good. Someone like Cortez or his hired thug came to mind. He'd started that way when Melinda's soft, hesitant voice filtered through the trees in the opposite direction, turning his blood to ice water. *What the hell is she doing out here?* Veering toward her instead, he moved with as much quiet stealth and speed as possible, praying she kept her mouth shut until he reached her.

Nick saw her flashlight beam right before he came up behind her on the narrow path. Transferring his flashlight to his slicker pocket, he snaked an arm around her, covering her mouth with his hand before she could call for him again, and put his lips against her ear. "*Shhh*. Someone else is out here." Her stiff body relaxed, and she nodded against his hold, signaling she understood. There would be time later to ask what she was doing looking for him; right now, he needed to get them both back to the cabin.

Thunder rumbled above the trees as he steered her in the opposite direction, the rain still coming down in sheets hard enough to penetrate the thick foliage and drench them. She, too, wore a rain slicker, which would help, but only so much against the heavy wind gusts.

"Good girl," he whispered in her ear as they reached the small clearing around the cabin, and she knew enough to remain quiet. "Run to the door."

Melinda didn't hesitate, just took off with him right behind her, shielding her in case whoever was stalking around was armed. She flung the door open, and he flinched, realizing she'd left it unlocked. As he maneuvered in front of her to enter first, someone called out from the trees.

"Hey, look, there's a cabin!"

Slamming the door behind them, he held onto the handle as he told her, "Stay put until I verify they aren't a threat."

Nick slipped back outside the same time two teens ran from the edge of the forest toward the door. Both halted in their tracks upon seeing him, and, when a lightning bolt lit the sky enough to glimpse their pale faces, he guessed their ages around thirteen or fourteen. He blew out a relieved breath that didn't lessen his annoyance at the scare they'd given him.

Injecting a note of authority in his tone, he asked, "What are you boys doing out here alone?" When they looked at each other with guilty expressions, he strode right up to them, not in the mood to play nice. "Don't even think about lying. I'm an ex-cop, and in no disposition to play guessing games tonight."

Their shoulders slumped, and the

freckle-faced one answered, "We snuck away from our troop, just for kicks, ya know? Then the storm came, and we got lost."

"Get in my truck, and don't argue. I'll take you back in a minute." He wasn't surprised they obeyed without delay. Nights turned cool in the mountains, even in the summer, and he guessed their shivering was due to being cold, wet, and scared. Nick pivoted and saw Melinda standing in the open door.

Saving his breath, he didn't bother taking the time to scold her. "Kids. I'll run them back to their camp and return. Lock the door."

She nodded, the light from the room behind her showing the concern etched on her face as she glanced toward his truck. "Okay. I hope they're all right."

"They are, but not deserving of your compassion. They scared the crap out of me when I thought it was someone stalking you."

Her soft lips twisted in a wry grin. "Me, too. I'll lock the door."

It took Nick over forty minutes to return the scouts to their troop and drive back to the cabin. He was tired and edgy from the panic that had gripped him when he thought Melinda was in danger and wasn't about to return to his tent or spend what was left of the night in his truck. If she didn't like it, too damn bad. He was bunking inside the cabin, and come morning, he would find a way to talk her into town or to stay at his place.

He rapped on the door, and she flung it open with the same stricken longing and need reflected in her clinging gaze as when he'd gone to her room that last night in the safehouse. Bracing himself to resist her, he entered and shut the door, reaching behind him to turn the lock. It took supreme effort to keep his eyes on her face and off the silky, sleeveless top that revealed the turgid outline of her nipples. The rain had dwindled to a steady fall, but the skies still boomed with thunder and lit up with jagged streaks of lightning. The stormy elements matched the roiling tempest brewing inside him.

Pulling the slicker over his head, he hung it on a peg next to hers, leaned against the door, and crossed his arms over his damp shirt. "The scare got to you, didn't it?" He couldn't help hoping that worked in his favor and she would now agree to leave this isolated location.

"Yes, some." When he raised a brow, she huffed and admitted, "Okay, yes, period." She stepped forward, her gaze never wavering, and placed a shaking hand on his rigid forearm, the light touch searing his flesh. "Maybe, if you're still willing to help me out, we could..."

Nick reacted fast so Melinda couldn't finish that sentence, spinning her around to take his place against the door. "Maybe I could pick up where we left off?" He lifted her arms above her head and shackled her delicate wrists with one hand. Her pulse leaped against his palm, her eyes going wide and dark, her nipples under the thin top hard enough to stab through his T-shirt.

"It's just tha it worked so well that night, but I don't want you to think it will change... *oh God*!" She gasped as he covered one breast with his hand and kneaded the soft, plump mound.

Thumbing her nipple, Nick dipped his head and nipped the soft skin of her neck, relishing another spike in her pulse. Her breathing hitched, but she didn't struggle in his hold, so he didn't think she was fretting over his dominant control. "Wouldn't change what?" Gripping her nipple, he applied slight pressure to the tender nub.

"What? Oh, um, you know, that I'm sending you mixed signals...*Nick*." She groaned as he suckled her nipple, the silk dampening from his mouth and tongue enough to cling to the tip when he raised his head.

Satisfied, he dropped his hands and stepped back, frowning. "I won't let you use me to settle your nerves when you refuse to trust me with your safety." He injected a note of sarcasm as he added, "What happened? Did you discover you wanted a taste of dangerous sex to alleviate boredom, or that you can trust me now?"

Shock, guilt, then anger flashed in her blue eyes before she shoved by him and stormed into the bedroom. She came out a minute later carrying a pillow and blanket and dumped them on the couch. "You can sleep there tonight."

Nick expected Melinda to slam the

bedroom door when she returned, but she shut it with a quiet click, and he didn't hear another sound from inside. Damn her for getting to him, and him for letting her.

****

Melinda leaned against the bedroom door, still feeling Nick's snug hold of her wrists, her body still hot and vibrating with need, wondering what it was about him that made her want him so much despite not fully trusting him. Hearing about Cortez's release, followed by seeing Nick again, had thrown her into a tailspin of conflicting, emotional upheaval, and she didn't know how to get off the roller-coaster ride. After tonight, though, she was certain of one thing – she wasn't cut out for or prepared to stay hidden from Cortez without help.

The storm had awoken her earlier, and her first thought and concern had been for Nick, stuck outside in the less-than-desirable elements. She tried for almost an hour to get back to sleep, telling herself he could either deal with it or pack up and go home. When that hadn't worked and guilt drove her from bed, she'd slipped on jeans and her parka and gone to check on him, having no real clear plan in mind. She still quaked from the fright he'd given her coming up behind her like that then pointing out someone was lurking around the cabin.

Stripping off her jeans, she crawled into bed with her body continuing to burn for his touch and pulled the covers over her head, the storm's grumbling lessening. She had no idea what kind of mood Nick would be in come morning, or how she would deal with him, only that she wasn't as safe alone as she had deluded herself into believing.

Melinda shoved her loose hair away from her face and gave Nick a disgruntled glare as she came out of the bedroom still groggy from too little sleep. "Why are you up so early?" She should have put her damp jeans back on instead of her old gym shorts that left her defenseless against his potent, dark-eyed perusal. How could he turn her into a puddle of hormone-driven, lustful need with one look when other men left her unmoved? His strong hold on her wrists, the way he'd taken control last night had awakened something inside her she couldn't define.

Nick shrugged and set the folded blanket on the couch. "I'm used to rising with the sun. I have animals that need tending and don't like to keep waiting. Plus, I have to get back and finish the preparations for the picnic this afternoon, the one I mentioned a few days ago. I told people about you, not anything about Cortez, just that you're a friend from my cop days, and they're hoping to meet you. Will you come, or do you still mistrust me enough to keep you from having fun in a safe environment around a lot of people?"

She was touched he would go to the trouble of mentioning her and wanted to go, so much it caused her a moment of indecision. She'd moved fast once before, without thinking through the possible consequences when she'd run to the cops after witnessing her father's murder.

"Would you trust everyone involved in my case, or who were aware of my whereabouts, if you were in my place?"

"Probably not." His stark, honest admission caught her unaware, as did the warm fuzzy filling her chest when he smiled. "What? Did you think I don't understand your fears?" Fisting his hands on his hips, his wide chest lifted with his deep inhale. He was a big man, towering over her five-foot-five, smaller frame, yet his size and strength had never intimidated her. "Look, Melinda. I get it, honest. I have two full-time employees, young men I never met until I moved here, if that makes you feel any better about staying with me after the picnic. If not, Jen said she can put you up at Miner's Junction. Either way, you'll be near other people who've never heard of Cortez, let alone would betray your whereabouts to him, or even a stranger passing through asking about you."

He made it sound so simple to decide, and considering what he'd said, she figured leaving the cabin was her best option. She kept going back to those weeks in the safehouse, how he'd gone out of his way to befriend her instead of treating the hours guarding her like a job. Mike and Owen were nice enough but had never taken that extra initiative to get to know who she was beyond a witness against a very bad man. That's what made

Nick stand out as both innocent and guilty.

Melinda strode past him into the kitchen and poured a cup of coffee, deciding she could think it to death and still wouldn't be 100 percent sure of him, regardless of meeting a slew of his closest friends. She couldn't afford the B&B for several weeks, especially not after losing the deposit on this cabin when she informed the rental she couldn't stay for the month she'd booked. If she ended up staying on his ranch, she would have the comfort of all those people knowing about her and him.

"Keep your friends close but your enemies closer."

Isn't that how the line went from *The Godfather II*? If she followed that advice, she would go against her father's last words to her mother.

Trust no one.

She hadn't heeded that caution when she'd gone to the cops, and look where she was now. Testing her decision to start with attending the picnic and go from there, she spun around when she heard him come up behind her. The same as every other time he was near, or even entered a room, her heart thudded in her chest, and her blood warmed. She'd lowered her guard around him enough to beg twice now, and she was still breathing. Maybe she could do it again without pleading for his touch and come away unscathed.

"For some reason, I think you're not quoting from *The Godfather* to test my movie knowledge."

Melinda didn't realize she'd spoken aloud but ignored his comment anyway. "I'll come to your picnic and tell you my decision about where I'll stay afterward. But just so you know, I've perfected my aim enough to take out all three cans, and I'm keeping my gun with me if I agree to your offer."

"Be my guest, and I mean that both literally and figuratively. How long will it take you to pack? I don't want to leave you alone up here for even a short time."

She smirked. "Not long since you're helping."

"In that case, you're helping with the picnic prep."

5

Chapter Six

Melinda followed Nick to his ranch, her gaze drawn to the wide expanse of rangeland spread beyond the stables and barn, the horses lazily grazing with tails swishing, the cattle drawn to a small lake shimmering under the midmorning sun. She'd always thought San Diego beautiful, the ocean and beaches as fun to visit as the mountains. It didn't take her long, though, to develop a deep appreciation for less traffic, fewer people, and the splendor of the West countryside. Whether it was driving past a wheat field blowing in the breeze, or a herd of graceful gazelle running by, or stopping for a moose and her baby to lumber across the road, she found pleasure in the stark differences between here and home.

And now there was much to like about

Nick's ranch, from the appealing farmhouse painted a dark beige with navy trim and shutters to match the outbuildings, to the array of picnic tables set up on the green lawn circling the house, to the friendly waves of two young men exiting the stable.

"That's Spenser and Jose." Nick jerked his head toward the two cowhands, reaching in the back seat of his truck to retrieve her largest bag. "I'll put this in the spare bedroom in case you decide to stay. Other than the perishables in your cooler, we can leave the rest of your belongings in the Jeep until after the picnic."

Before she could say anything, he went inside, leaving her standing there alone with his employees who approached with friendly smiles.

"Ma'am." The tall, lanky blond tipped his hat. "Welcome. I'm Spenser, and this is Jose." He nodded toward the shorter, stockier, dark-haired man who also nudged his hat in greeting. "Can we carry something inside for you?"

"I'm Melinda, and no, but thanks. I only have a small cooler that's going in right now."

"You need anything while you're here, just ask. One of us is always around." Spenser glanced over at Nick as he came down the porch steps. "Hey, boss. The sheriff and a couple of others dropped off the tables and put food in the kitchen, like you said they might. Are they set up the way you want?"

"They look good, thanks, guys. Give me a minute to show Melinda around then we'll get the horseshoes and volleyball net set up."

Melinda was backing out of the rear seat of her Jeep, holding the cooler handles, and bumped into Nick, her butt hitting his groin. She jumped and sidestepped away from that brief press against his thick bulge before turning. Averting her gaze, she hoped her face wasn't flaming like the blood rushing through her veins.

"I'll take that." Nick took the cooler from her and jerked his head toward the house. "Come on in, and I'll help you get this stuff in the refrigerator."

She was a little miffed he appeared unaffected by that butt/groin bump until they reached the front door and he leaned down to whisper, "Good thing you have a soft ass, or I'd be hurting right now."

She chuckled, pleased he'd noticed. "Keep it up and you might still get hurt."

He sighed, entering the house behind her. "Promises, promises."

This was the detective Melinda remembered, good at teasing her out of her moods, easing her worry or testiness when the lockdown got to her. The refinished hardwood floors were spread throughout the living, dining, and kitchen areas, but as she followed him into the kitchen, she noticed the remodeling didn't stop with the floors. "Your kitchen is a mess," she commented, looking at the lack of countertops and the stripped upper cabinets waiting for the same walnut stain already on the lowers.

"The whole house is a work in progress." Nick set the cooler on the tabletop and gestured to the refrigerator. "Since I haven't cooked much, your stuff will fit. The trays of meat are for the grill this afternoon. I have to get outside and finish setting up before people start arriving around one. Make yourself at home."

"How many are you expecting? Maybe I

can make a dish. I'm a decent cook."

"I remember. As far as how many, I have no idea, I didn't ask for RSVPs. They'll show up carrying a dish or they won't."

A wave of nostalgia hit Melinda. She'd often fixed meals for everyone in the safehouse, sometimes out of boredom, other times when she tired of fast food. Nick would always offer to help, and she'd enjoyed brushing against him as they moved around the small space trying to stump each other with movie trivia. She doubted she would have fared as well during those long weeks of confinement without the extra effort he'd exerted to make them bearable.

He shocked the hell out of her when he paused on his way out to grip her chin and hold her head up for a quick kiss. "It was fun cooking with you."

Melinda watched him walk away, her lips tingling, her body craving more while she questioned what he wanted from her other than to trust him again. She couldn't bring herself to take that risk yet, regardless of how she went damp from one look or light touch, but she yearned for a return of their friendly, easy banter.

She unloaded the cooler then retrieved a pair of shorts from the bag Nick left on the sofa. After changing, she ventured outside to see if she could help with anything, but several vehicles were already parked in the long drive, and a group of tall, Stetson-wearing cowboys were assisting Nick.

Sitting down on the top porch step, she watched him lead two horses to a corral rail, looking as at home hefting a saddle onto one as he had checking the surveillance cameras around the safehouse. It didn't take long to realize how well this new life he'd chosen suited him. She couldn't deny the rancher appealed to her as much as the detective once had, or that she risked her heart as well as her safety if she couldn't bring herself to trust him.

"We meet again."

Melinda switched her gaze from Nick's broad shoulders to the pregnant blonde walking up to the porch. Recognizing her as the same woman who had befriended her at the candle shop, she returned her greeting. "So we do. I'm Melinda," she replied, coming to her feet.

"Lisa McDuff." She pointed to the only other person Melinda recognized, the sheriff. "That's my husband, Shawn. He mentioned you two met."

"Yes, at the beginning of the week." She left it at that, not privy to what Nick told everyone about her. "This sounds like a big deal, and a lot of work."

"Not so much a big deal – we enjoy impromptu get-togethers, and there's plenty of help. Skye and I are in charge of the beverage table. Would you like to join us?"

Glad for the diversion from ogling Nick, she nodded. "Sure. Lead the way." Melinda eyed Lisa's large abdomen. "When are you due?"

She smiled, rubbing her stomach. "A few weeks, and he can't come soon enough. We've set up under the red oak for shade. Do you remember Skye?" Lisa gestured toward the woman with the same midnight hair color as Melinda.

"Yes. The candle you recommended smelled wonderful. I think I burned it down within a few days," Melinda said as they reached the table under the towering oak. Compared to California heat, the warm days here were quite pleasant. Regardless of the mild temperature, she welcomed the shade the tree offered.

"Anna Lee will love hearing that. It means repeat customers. You're Melinda, Nick's guest," Skye guessed.

"For the afternoon, yes." Lisa and Skye exchanged a look of disappointment that prompted Melinda to ask, "What?"

Lisa's expression turned sheepish. "We were hoping, since he planned this to introduce you to everyone, that there was more to your relationship."

A jolt went through her. "He said that, that he planned this for me?" Why would he do such a thing and then not tell her? "He told me picnics were held all summer long."

"They are, but the one for this month was three weeks ago, and the next one planned isn't for another two weeks, and the whole town and surrounding residents are invited to those. Nick's been a difficult man to get to know, so we were all pleased he suggested hosting one just for us. He's kept to himself a lot since moving here last year, which, of course, tickles our curiosity."

That didn't sound like the man Melinda remembered. He'd been open and outgoing from the moment they'd met, with her and with his colleagues. "What has he told you about us?" she inquired, grabbing a bag of ice and upending it into the large ice chest while they filled the iced tea and lemonade jugs.

"Nothing, which is typical of Nick." Skye shifted her gaze toward Nick who was securing a volleyball net with Shawn's help. "The strong, silent type always sends my mind racing with ideas."

When Melinda frowned, wondering what she meant, Lisa cleared her throat and stated, "Skye's an author. She's always looking for inspiration for her male characters."

Her name didn't sound familiar, but Melinda couldn't remember one author from another. "What do you write? Maybe I've read something by you."

As she'd hoped, their discussion turned to books and kept her from answering questions about her relationship with Nick.

But, like a dog with a bone, they returned to the topic when they'd finished readying the drink table and more people were arriving.

Skye opened a package of paper cups, glancing at Melinda. "We know Nick's from Cheyenne. Did you two meet at a club there?"

"Club? Like a bar or nightclub? No." She questioned the disappointment reflected on their faces. "Another answer you weren't expecting?"

Lisa shook her head as they walked toward the house. "Sorry, it's not that. Since he's been here, he's played the field without an interest in seeing anyone beyond a time or two at a club we all frequent. You come as a surprise."

"We met in Cheyenne when Nick was working on a case. Our meeting up again was an odd coincidence, that's all." She was confident no one here had heard of Cortez, but the less people knew of her, the safer she would stay. Several people were putting covered dishes on the food table, everyone chatting like long-time friends. Melinda experienced a stab of loneliness, which didn't make sense with all these people around. "I should grab my deviled eggs from the kitchen," she said, needing a few minutes alone. "If there's anything else I can do, let me know."

"Want to partner with me in the three-legged relay?" Skye asked, nodding toward Lisa. "There's no way she can hop in a race."

"There's no way I can do a lot of things anymore," Lisa grumbled. "Like see my feet."

Shawn walked up behind her and wrapped an arm around her between belly and breasts. Melinda caught the subtle glide of his thumb over a nipple, a shudder rippling down her spine imaging the pleasure of such a touch from a man she was comfortable and confident enough with to let him get away with such a thing in front of others.

"They're still there," he stated with humor. Glancing at Melinda, he smiled. "Ms. Walsh, I'm glad Nick convinced you to come today. I hope we see more of you."

In other words, he hoped Melinda would take Nick up on his offer of staying on the ranch. "It should be fun. Skye, come find me when it's time for the race."

Crossing the lawn, she saw Nick astride

a black horse, holding a squealing toddler in front of him as they rode around a corral. Not once during the two months she'd seen him almost every day had she pictured him with a kid, yet, looking at him now, he appeared a natural with the young boy. Eager to talk to him about his motives for today, she dashed inside and put her tray of deviled eggs on top of a pan filled with ice to keep them cool. They probably weren't the smartest choice to bring to an outdoor picnic even with the moderate low eighties temperature and slight breeze that kept the air pleasant. But given the disarray of Nick's kitchen and the limited options, it was the best she could come up with at the last minute.

Which made Melinda wonder when he decided to plan this for her, and why.

****

Nick dismounted with the Carsons' son clutched in his arm. The kid loved riding, his high-pitched screeches still ringing in Nick's ears. Nancy Carson held out her arms for her son, her smile as proud as his.

"Thank you, Nick. I would only trust a few people with Joey's welfare."

The local veterinarian and his wife had visited Spurs once since he'd joined, their two young children keeping them home Anson Carson told him once when he'd been out to tend a wounded horse. "I'm glad I'm among them. He's not too young to start riding lessons, and I think some stables have a few Shetlands to start the little ones out with. I'm sure Anson knows which ones." Noticing Melinda heading his way, he tipped his hat. "Enjoy the afternoon, Darcy."

"You have a great turnout, and that food looks good. Catch you later."

Leaning against the corral fence, Nick hooked his right boot heel on the lower rail and bent his elbows to brace his arms on the top. He kept his hat lowered because Melinda was too good at reading his expressions, and he didn't doubt the churning need tightening his body was reflected on his face. Want was too mild to describe the ache he'd carried for her since they first met at his precinct. Her wide blue eyes had reflected the horror and fear of witnessing her father's murder, but a determined glint accompanied her forceful insistence on testifying, even after the risks were laid out for her.

He would have committed several ethical violations if he'd seduced her back then. As it was, he'd crossed a line that last night, one he didn't regret, not then, and not now, considering her mistrust was keeping them from picking up where they'd left off.

Now here she was, coming toward him with those long legs he'd fantasized wrapped around him closing the gap, the look on her face curious with a hint of doubt. His cock jerked, and his palm itched, wishing he could haul her into the tack room, bend her over a sawhorse, shove those shorts down, and take her mind off her worries. From the way her nipples peaked under her thin tee, her body was on board with his thinking, but, from her face, her mind was still wallowing in distrust.

"You're good with kids," she said, halting in front of him. In her sneakers, her head came to his chest, and she craned her neck to glance under his hat. "You're also good at keeping secrets. Lisa and Skye told me you planned this impromptu gathering for me.

Why?"

Nick removed the straw sprig he was chewing on and tossed it on the ground before thumbing his Stetson up. "I would think the answer obvious, but then you're so distrustful, you can't see what's right in front of you." He saw the moment the lightbulb went off in her head.

"You planned all this"—she waved her arm behind her—"so everyone would know if I decided to stay here."

"Exactly. If you went missing, who do you think would be the number one suspect? The sheriff knows about Cortez, but I didn't give him any details on your ordeal other than all four of us were betrayed by a mole. Neither you, I, Mike, nor Owen walked away that night unscathed." He kept his eyes on hers as he reached out and traced a finger over the scar on her forehead. "You don't hide your physical pain, only your hurt from whoever's to blame. It wasn't me."

Melinda bit her lip, her eyes getting watery until she blinked the tears away. "What am I going to do with you?"

"I can give you several suggestions, but

how about you start today with having some fun." He pushed away from the fence and slung an arm around her shoulders. "Let's eat and play games. No pressure. You can either unpack in the guest room tonight or work out something with Jen at her place."

"I'll stay here, but I want to learn to ride, and you have to get at least one countertop on so I can cook. I'm going to come and go as I please. You're my host this time, not my guard. And I'm not staying past the month I planned, two weeks now. I have a life in San Diego. It's nice here, the people are friendly, but it's not home."

"And there's no place like home?"

Her smile erased the confused sadness in her eyes. "Maybe for Dorothy in 1939. For me?" She shrugged. "We'll see. Do you agree to my terms?"

"Teaching you to ride and installing a countertop, yes. We can discuss the rest later," he returned, not willing to concede to all of her demands. Her safety had been paramount for him, Mike, and Owen last time. Under the circumstances, this time around he wouldn't chance her welfare to anyone else.

Nick's gratitude for his new friends rose exponentially that afternoon as they welcomed Melinda without bombarding her with nosy questions. He watched her relax more and more with each introduction, every invitation to socialize, and even the teasing innuendos about their relationship.

"I'm glad your appetite is the same," he commented when she finished a full plate of food with all the relish and gusto he remembered.

"I never let anything interfere with me and food, especially dessert." She pushed her big plate away and drew two smaller pie plates forward. "Cherry or lemon first?"

"I couldn't decide on pie, so I grabbed the brownies." The strawberry blonde set the baby carrier on the bench and held a hand out to Melinda. "I'm Mickie Daniels. Don't believe a word of anything my husband says about me."

"Believe every word. I'm Randy."

Melinda grinned, glancing between the two then peeking around Mickie at the baby. "He's adorable."

Mickie's gray eyes softened when she gazed down at her son. "I think so, but thanks."

Nick turned to Randy, bringing his beer to his mouth for a long swallow before saying, "Thanks for coming. I finally get the chance to meet your little guy. Tyson, right?"

"Correct. And I get to check out your girl. Welcome to Idaho, Melinda." Randy held out a large hand.

She shook his hand, shooting her gaze toward Nick, as if expecting him to refute Randy's assumption. He left it up to her since he wasn't sure what she was to him yet. "Thank you, and I'm not his girl. We're just friends."

Mickie burst out laughing. "Boy, does that sound familiar. Only *he*"—she pointed her fork across the table at her husband—"used to be the annoying, overprotective brother I never wanted. Be warned, Melinda, the guys around here can turn overbearing when they get in protection mode."

She sent Nick a teasing grin. "I'm a decent shot and can take care of myself."

"That remains to be proven," Nick

retorted just as Skye came over, reminding him he was due to spell Clayton on the grill.

"Sack race time, Melinda. Hey, Mickie. Oh, he's so cute." She crooned to the baby as Melinda pushed her pies toward Nick.

"Watch them, don't eat them," she ordered.

"Can't. I'm needed on the grill." He handed the pies to Randy and Mickie. "We'll get more after the race. Catch you two later."

"Have fun," Randy returned.

Nick could see the three-legged relays from the grill on the back patio and chuckled when Skye and Melinda took off, hobbling on their sacked legs, laughing like schoolgirls. Melinda's face glowed with pleasure, the same as when he'd brought her to climax all those months ago yet could remember with vivid clarity. He wanted that relief mechanism for her again, as much for her as for him. He didn't savor the idea of walking around with a hard-on for his guest the next few weeks, but, until she gave him her full trust, he wouldn't pursue more.

With difficulty, he tamped down the urge to hover and turned his attention to the grill, waiting until the afternoon had wound down and people were leaving to go in search of her again. He found her leaning against the back fence, looking at the grazing horses, and rested his arms on the top rail next to hers.

"They're beautiful animals, aren't they?" she stated without glancing at him, her tone carrying a wistful note.

"I've always thought so." He pointed to Ghost. "The dapple gray is my personal mount, Ghost. I brought him and the other gray with me from Cheyenne, where I boarded them at a stable. They love it here."

"I'll bet, and I can tell from your voice how much you care for your horses." She looked toward Merry, standing alone under a tree. "That brown one is pretty. What... *oh*!" Melinda's hand went to her throat, her voice conveying soft pity when Merry turned her head and she could see her cratered, damaged neck. "What happened?"

"She's a wild mustang rescue, so best guess by the vet is she tangled with an aggressive stallion. The wound was infected when they found her, and there was doubt she would survive. But she's got an iron will." He turned a sardonic grin on Melinda. "Merry doesn't trust me yet, either, or anyone else for that matter."

Melinda's soft lips curled, tempting him to go caveman on her. Luckily, he still possessed enough restraint to resist.

"Smart girl."

"Merry or you?" he asked, not sure who she meant.

"Merry. The jury's still out on my intellect when it comes to you. I'll help clean up."

Nick fell in step with her as they walked over to the tables. "Just be smart enough not to get close to Merry. She's not of a mind to make nice with anyone just yet."

****

The quiet click of the front door closing caught Nick's attention as he came out of his bathroom wearing only his jeans and boots. Glancing out the window that faced the front, he could barely make out Melinda walking toward the stable in the dark. She'd seemed restless when he told her good night an hour ago but swore she didn't need Spenser or Jose to stay in the loft room above the barn for her peace of mind, that she was fine now that so many people were aware she was staying with him.

Nick didn't hesitate to follow her. Whether she liked it or not, she was his responsibility as much here on his ranch as when he'd been assigned her case in Cheyenne. He went still hearing her soft voice when he entered the stable then peered down the middle aisle dividing the stalls. Perched on a hay bale across from Merry's stall, she sat with one leg drawn up, her arm wrapped around her knee, her head resting against the wood gate behind her.

"I get it, sweetie. Men can be brutes, can't they? I hope you got in a nip or two to the guy who hurt you. I didn't. Nope, they ganged up on me, one holding me down, the other..." She paused, and his heart twisted when she spoke again with a painful catch in her voice. "Let's just say he enjoyed his work way too much."

Merry bobbed her head up and down, whinnying as if she understood and commiserated.

"Yeah, you understand, don't you? I knew you would. I wish I could hug you, but Nick says you wouldn't like that. Can't blame you." She dropped her leg and leaned forward, putting her head down in her hands, but Nick could still hear her when she mumbled, "I couldn't let anyone near me until I saw your new owner again." She glanced up to tell the mare, "You would like his touch, Merry. No one can make the fear go away like Nick."

He couldn't help himself. Nick strode down the aisle and, when she whipped her head around, he stated, "I changed my mind. You can use me all you want to exorcise your demons, whether you can give me your full trust or not."

Chapter Seven

It took a moment for Nick's words to register, and a split second afterward for Melinda to go hot and wet. Coming to her feet, she sucked in a breath when he halted in front of her, close enough his body heat penetrated her clothes and she could see the stark desire reflected in his dark eyes. Less than two weeks ago, she'd threatened to shoot him if he came near her, unsure who she could trust from that debacle in Cheyenne. Now she was more befuddled by the lengths he'd taken to worm his way past her defenses, and why.

She'd enjoyed the picnic and his friends, and, when she'd learned he planned it for her sake, to ease her mind about staying here, the last of her misgivings had crumbled. She managed to hold herself together while they cleaned up, to ignore the lust his nearness and searing glances always ignited.

The mare had drawn her compassion earlier, and Melinda had glimpsed a kindred spirit in her doe eyes. Edgy sleeplessness had driven her to the stable when she'd found Nick's nearness in the house too distracting, her craving for his touch to take her away from reality for a spell growing in leaps and bounds. It took a lot to make her uncomfortable, but now she fidgeted under his intense regard, wondering how much Nick had heard when she was wallowing in a rare bout of self-pity while talking to Merry.

"You're not the type to let yourself be used for anything, and I don't want your pity." It was either get to the bottom of this unexpected offer or make a fool of herself by stripping off her clothes.

Nick gave her one of his sexy grins, his eyes tracing her features before sliding down to her braless breasts, her nipples puckered against the soft cotton tee. Reaching up, he cupped one breast and leaned forward, his firm touch and soft brush of his lips over hers snagging her breath, possibly her sanity.

"When you have that look on your face, the one that says you're tired of carrying your burdens alone, I can be anything you need. And I don't pity you; I admire the hell out of you."

He took her mouth in a slow kiss, and Melinda opened under the pressure, groaning in surrender. His hard strength warmed her cold insides, his thumb abrading her nipple heated her entire breast, and his exploring tongue tracing her gums and dueling with hers spread fire down to her toes. Locking his free arm around her lower back, he pulled her pelvis against the rigid shape of his cock, and she went up in flames. Melinda clutched his broad shoulders, wanting him and struggling with yearning for him to just take her, fuck her until nothing mattered except the pleasure, nothing scared her except how much she needed him.

Nick kept kissing her, driving her senseless with his mouth and tongue, grinding his cock against her mound, his jeans and her thin gym shorts worthless barriers against the hot friction. *Wow* was all her muddled brain could come up with. When he decided to take over, it was devastating to any thought of telling herself this was just sex.

Barely able to draw a breath, she tore her mouth from his, her throat catching as she gazed at the raw lust stamped on his rugged face, the dark need swirling in his eyes when he whipped her top over her head. "Nick." Melinda leaned into the hand now cupping her bare breast, the pleasure of his calloused palm scraping her sensitive skin making her forget they were in a stable.

"Tell me," he demanded, pinching her nipple. "Am I getting you off, or am I taking this further than before?"

"Do you always ask instead of seducing?"

He bent his head and nipped her bottom lip, the slight sting sending a lightning bolt straight to her nipples. "I'm polite." When she huffed a laugh, he turned serious again and pinned her with a direct stare. "You trust me now, and I don't want to lose that gift. I can give you what you need if that's all you want."

Melinda made the snap decision that

only here and now mattered and could think of only one thing to say after that. "I want you."

"You have me." Grasping her shoulders, he turned her toward the hay bale and nudged her down. "Bend over."

Her heart slammed against her chest as she braced her hands on the soft but scratchy hay, the straw's sweet aroma helping defuse the more pungent odors in the stalls. She quaked, inside and out, when he lowered her shorts and panties, dropping them at her feet before using his booted foot to nudge her feet wider apart. Cooler air wafted over her exposed flesh, eliciting goose bumps and shivers of awareness at her exposure.

"Do you still want this?" he asked, bracing a hand on the bale next to hers and leaning over her to cup one breast with the other hand. Melinda moaned with the scrape of his nail across her tender nipple, back to wishing he would act instead of ask.

All it took was turning her face to his and encountering his heated, dark-eyed stare to strip away the last of her insecurities and doubts, much the same as when she first met him and he had assured her he would keep her safe. "Yes." Melinda arched into his hand to emphasize her answer, heat spiraling to her pussy as he plucked at the distended bud with tight pinches.

She whimpered from the pleasure/pain, the pitiful sound of need slipping out as she pressed her butt against his denim-covered thighs. "Nick, *please.*"

Melinda dropped her head. So much for not begging again.

"Like that, do you?" he murmured in her ear, releasing her throbbing tip and shifting over to her other dangling breast.

Biting her lip, Melinda looked down at his sun-kissed hand against her whiter skin then closed her eyes against the scorching pleasure of those clever fingers plucking her nipple. Thankfully, he didn't demand an answer. She doubted she could form a coherent thought as he lavished much-needed attention on her nipples, alternating between them until she panted with escalating lust for more.

"Nick." She couldn't think beyond saying his name.

"I love that needy catch in your voice."

Nick released her breast and straightened, running his hands down her bowed back in a slow caress that ended with him palming her buttocks.

She clenched her hands in the hay and gritted her teeth. "If you stop now, I'll shoot you," she warned, and that wasn't an idle threat. Whether it was him she craved with such fiery intensity or the stress of keeping herself safe that was responsible for her heightened arousal, she didn't know or care. All she wanted was the sweet oblivion of release to take her away from reality for a while.

"Maybe I shouldn't have encouraged you to hone your shooting skills."

He delivered a sharp smack to her right buttock, startling her when the burning sting proved more arousing than painful. She sucked in a breath, swiveling her head around to gape at him. "What was that for?"

"My pleasure." He caressed the throbbing area, and she shuddered with the pleasure coursing through her. "And from the look on your face, yours, too." Keeping his eyes on her face, he swatted her other cheek, the initial hot pain morphing into a sweet pulse of arousal she couldn't deny when he ran his fingers over the spot and asked, "Is this the first time someone has spanked you?"

"Yes. I am a grown woman, you know." She shouldn't find a painful smack arousing, exciting, should she? Wasn't that wrong on several levels?

Nick smirked, kneading her buttocks. "I'm well aware of that. Just because it's different or new, doesn't mean it's wrong, Melinda. But we have time to discuss that more later." He slid two fingers down her crack and into her pussy.

Melinda moaned, dropping her head back down, embracing the distraction from that comment as she relished the stretch and burn of his deep-fingered thrust. Closing her eyes, she shifted her upthrust hips against his pummeling hand, quivering from the steady abrasion against her clit and the heated flashes and convulsive spasms his strokes ignited. Her mind went numb to everything but the pleasure, her brain fogging as he glided the pad of his rough thumb up between her cheeks and teased her anus. She tried coming out of the stupor to protest, but just like before when he'd ventured back there, she wasn't strong enough to stall the lust consuming her to cope with a minor uncertainty. The ache for that sweet oblivion she remembered so well and had been craving kept command of her senses. It wasn't until the small clutches heralding the onset of an orgasm began and he slowly removed his fingers that she could find her voice to protest.

"*No!* Don't...not yet. *Please.*" She cringed at the pathetic plea but couldn't seem to help herself.

"I've waited two years to get inside you," Nick stated in a guttural tone as he lifted her around and sat her bare butt down on the straw. The pressure emphasized the burn from his swats, her pussy spasming with an emptiness she yearned for him to fill.

She'd been so immersed in spiraling arousal she hadn't heard him don a condom with his free hand. Zeroing in on his jutting cock, her heart pounded in anticipation, her thighs falling open when he scooped his hands under her cheeks and lifted her pelvis. Falling back to brace on her hands, she wrapped her legs around his back and whispered, "*Yes*," watching as he glided between her swollen labia and worked his thick length inside her inch by slow inch.

"I guess I don't have to ask how you're doing since your face and body are speaking loud and clear. Deep breath, Melinda."

She inhaled as he surged inside her, stretching unused muscles and rasping over long-neglected nerve endings in one fell swoop. Her gaze drifted from their connected groins up his ridged abdomen, over his wide chest decorated with a light smattering of black curls, to his sun-darkened, intense face. She almost climaxed from the sheer carnality of his expression and in his eyes. Needing more than the slow withdrawal once he'd buried himself deep, she tried arching toward him, and, when his firm hold on her hips prevented that, she squeezed her inner muscles, attempting to hold him inside her. As with everything else, she couldn't win against his strength, and he slipped free, leaving her empty again.

"Damn it, Nick, quit toying with me."

Melinda choked up, so desperate for release she wanted to cry or hit him over the head with a board.

"You're tight. I don't want to hurt you. Trust me to know what I'm doing, darlin'. Say yes and follow my lead, or no, and we can still end this."

The dark commanding tone of his rough voice tugged at her nipples, prompted her sheath to gush with anticipation. He asked again for her trust, but hadn't she already given it to him? She was here, on his ranch, with no one else around now, and not once since everyone departed had she felt threatened, unsafe, or even unsure of him.

Her answer slipped out without having to think it over. "Yes."

He smiled with satisfaction, sliding back inside her, thrusting faster as her muscles loosened, taking her over with his deep plunges and intent focus on her and her needs. This was what she craved, someone who knew what she wanted and needed better than she, to take command and leave her no choice but to go with the flow or end it and walk away unsatisfied. With each harder, deeper thrust, the past receded a little more. Every time he withdrew, stopping with her folds wrapped only around his cockhead before filling her again, she didn't have to think about tomorrow. Only now mattered.

Nick pulled back and then set up a steady rhythm that robbed her of breath and coherent thought. Melinda arched her torso like a bow under his pistoning hips, her pussy clamping around his steely erection, the spasming muscles too slippery to hold him inside her. Her breathing grew ragged as he went deeper, pounded harder between her gripping thighs. The orgasmic contractions grew stronger, tingling pleasure starting to ripple deep inside her core, and he locked her groin so close to his, he couldn't withdraw but an inch or two. His face was as hard as his cock, his concentration fierce and exciting, those chocolate eyes in constant motion, sliding from her face down to their connected bodies and then back up to her face.

Melinda blushed, something she rarely did, but *God*, the position, his look, and pleasure was so carnal, she couldn't help herself. In this position, everything was right *there*, open and on display for both of them to see. In between his now short, jabbing thrusts and her face, her perspiration-shiny breasts jiggled, the reddened tips puckered into tight, upthrusting pinpoints. His focused attention, not only between her legs where her folds clung to his pumping cock but also checking on her expressions, made it easy to fantasize he cared for her, in some way. Her pussy quivered around his cock, heat blurring her vision, and she gave herself over to the euphoric bliss.

****

"Now, Melinda," Nick ground out, sinking balls deep inside her slick pussy, unable to hold back any longer. Her damp muscles squeezed and massaged his thick girth with her climax, the friction incredibly hot as she bathed him with her creamy release. He loved seeing her arch her head back, close her eyes, her face suffused with pleasure and free of worry. Letting go with his own orgasm, he groaned at the hot pleasure sweeping up from his balls to spew into the latex, his head stuck in a euphoric fog for several moments before he came down from the high with slower dips inside her snug, rippling body.

"Darlin', I think you may have scorched me." Nick kissed her soft lips, fast and hard. She dropped her legs with a contented sigh and opened her eyes, the blue depths conveying the same sated pleasure still tingling through his body.

A small grin hovered around her lips. "*Mmmm*, it would serve you right for dragging it out. FYI – I'm good with quickies."

"Good to know, since I take that to mean we're not going to return to the house and go to separate rooms."

Melinda sat up with a jerk, her face turning even redder. Reaching for her top lying at his feet, she stuttered, "I didn't mean...the guest bedroom is fine...I don't want to put you out."

Nick dropped the condom in the trash and yanked his jeans up but left them open to take the top from her hand. Pulling it over her head, he decided he liked her wearing nothing but a thigh-skimming T-shirt with nothing underneath and scooped up her shorts before she could get to them.

"You'll put me out if you *don't* sleep with me." She glared when he kept her from taking the shorts and reached behind her to slip under the shirt and pinch her ass. "Behave. Tomorrow we can discuss boundaries, what I expect, how far you're willing to go." Hoisting her over his shoulder, he rested his palm on her buttock as he strode toward the door, Merry's neigh echoing in the stable behind them.

"I'll come back, Merry," Melinda called out, sliding a hand down into his loosened pants to pinch his butt.

"Shit! Knock it off before I drop you."

"Then you knock it off, and what's with the caveman routine?"

She wasn't fighting him, and her breathless tone hinted she liked either his hold, her bare butt exposure, that pinch, or all of the above.

"All men are cavemen at heart. We can discuss that tomorrow, too. I'm too tired tonight."

"Okay," she agreed as he entered the house. "But you're not getting your way with everything."

Striding down the hall, he caressed her cheeks then her slit, finding her wet again. "We'll see."

Nick awoke at the crack of dawn, like usual, but this time to the pleasure of snuggling up against Melinda's soft ass. It took less than a second to decide he wouldn't mind waking up every morning for a good long while like this. Taking a peek at her face, he sighed seeing the dark circles under her eyes. He'd ridden her hard last night, but he guessed it was her restless sleep that accounted for the signs of fatigue. As much as he didn't want to, it might be best if he refrained from sex for a few days, until she acclimated to staying with him and built up enough faith in their relationship to gain confidence of her safety.

He disengaged from her body and rolled out of bed. Grabbing his clothes off a corner chair, he padded into the hall bath to shower and dress. When he checked on her afterward and found her still abed, he went to start the coffee and see what he could put together for breakfast. Gazing at his half-finished kitchen, he decided he would tackle a countertop this morning before going out on his scheduled appointments after lunch. With the kitchen table holding small appliances like the coffee maker and microwave, there was little prep space. He'd gotten by with grilling, using paper plates, and eating on the patio, and they might have to continue in that vein for a few days.

After witnessing the ease and skill with which Melinda gutted fish for dinner and her camping experience, she wouldn't balk at that. He liked how self-sufficient she was, both when living in comfort and roughing it in the woods. But, remembering the meals she would fix for the four of them, he looked forward to making some space for her to cook.

An hour later, he heard her moving about and looked up from measuring the longest counter when she entered the kitchen. "Good morning." Her hair was still loose, hanging past her shoulders, the black waves a sharp contrast emphasizing the bright blue of her eyes. She wore the same gym shorts with a different tee, and he liked she went for comfort instead of style.

"It will be if what I'm smelling tastes half as good. How long have you been up?" Her eyes flickered toward the coffeepot on the table.

"Awhile." He jerked his head toward the coffee. "Help yourself to anything you want or need. Not that I have much in the kitchen. Just the basics. Pillsbury cinnamon rolls was the best I could do, and I have eggs, if you want."

He looked for signs of lingering discomfort or any other adverse effects from his rough fucking last night, but she moved with ease and appeared relaxed. His struggle to work himself inside her tight pussy signaled a long absence from sex, and he wondered if her trauma in Cheyenne was to blame, or something else had held her back all this time.

Melinda poured a cup of coffee then looked in the refrigerator and took out the milk and eggs. "I'll whip up some scrambled eggs if you have a skillet handy."

"I do." He pulled one out of a lower cabinet and set it on the stove. "No fresh spinach, but there's an onion and cheese in there."

"You remembered?" she asked, appearing surprised he could recall the extras she would add to scrambled eggs at the safehouse.

"I remember everything about you." Leaning against the counter, he watched her chop the onion and whip the eggs with milk on the table. "Why did you go out to the stable last night?" he asked when she turned to the stove and he glimpsed the same sorrow on her face as he'd seen last night when she was talking to Merry.

"I couldn't sleep thinking about her, what she went through, and..." She paused, averting her face, concentrating on stirring the eggs.

"And the similarity with your trauma?"

"Are you into psychoanalysis, now?" she retorted, her shoulders stiffening.

"It doesn't take a degree in psychology to see the correlation, and don't get testy, Melinda. I'm glad you kept your distance.

Merry is unpredictable."

"She's sweet. You can see it in her eyes, her fear and need for understanding without the pity. These are ready."

Nick's heart went out to her. She put on a good front, acting like her scars didn't bother her, hiding behind her mistrust over the failure to find the person who had betrayed her. It had taken a strong person to go up against Cortez after witnessing his brutal retaliation methods, and to endure such a terror-filled, painful ordeal with such stoic resolve. She might stumble now and then, but he would make sure no one caused her to fall.

"Here." He handed her paper plates to scoop the eggs while he retrieved the cinnamon rolls. "We can eat outside. It's nice this morning." When they'd settled at the table, he said, "I can take you riding later today, if you want. After I get a countertop on, I have two farrier jobs. Spenser and Jose are here if you need anything; otherwise, feel free to explore." He hesitated then added, "I prefer you stick close, within hearing range of my hands."

Melinda frowned then seemed to hold back whatever rebuke was on the tip of her tongue. "I planned to, so no problem. You do know the odds of Cortez finding me here are slim to none. I haven't told anyone my whereabouts except you."

"I won't trust your safety to odds. You haven't gone out much since returning home, have you?"

Her gaze turned wary at his quick change of subject, but what better way to divert her attention from Cortez and his threats than interesting her into broadening her sexual experience?

"Why do you think that?"

"Because you haven't had sex in a while."

Nick could tell she didn't care for his blunt observation, but her acceptance, and the way she embraced his control with wholehearted enthusiasm were small signs of sexual submission he would love to explore further.

Melinda's face heated under Nick's intense regard and straightforward, observant remark, but she didn't bother denying the truth. He was too in tune with her to try to get away with a lie. "What gave it away, or do I want to know?"

His mouth curled in one of those sexy, melt-your-panties grins. "Your tight pussy."

She damn near choked on her cinnamon roll but, when she finally swallowed, she couldn't keep from chuckling. "I guess I asked for that. There's nothing wrong with abstaining now and then, and I don't jump into bed with just anyone. But if you think I need to get out more, tell me about the local club where everyone hangs out around here."

He closed his mouth instead of taking the bite of eggs on his raised fork, eyeing her across the table with a curious look. Setting down his utensil, he cocked his head, asking, "Who mentioned a nearby club?"

"I don't know. I think it was Lisa. What does it matter?" She found his speculative perusal over a simple question odd.

"She didn't tell you what kind of club, huh?"

Amusement lurked in his gaze, and Melinda was starting to grow annoyed. What was the big deal? "Fine, if you don't want to discuss it for whatever ridiculous reason, I'll ask Spenser or Jose." She stood and reached for her plate, but he shackled her wrist, her pulse skyrocketing from his light grip and his thumb caressing her throbbing vein.

"Spurs is a private club catering to those who participate in alternative sexual practices. Still interested?"

Melinda slowly sat back down, surprised, and yet, somehow, not shocked he would be involved with alternative sex. His control, the way he held her immobile in the safehouse, at the cabin, and last night, and how he could take her over with a look or few words and a touch had hinted at a dominant nature she now understood better.

An odd quiver of longing rippled through her and, to cover up her confusion, her voice came out tart with a touch of humor when she replied, "You're into tying up your girlfriends and spanking them?"

Nick pushed up, leaned over the table, and cupped her head to draw her face up for a hard, commanding kiss that increased her craving for more of him and the unknown. "I don't have girlfriends but enjoy bondage and spanking a delectable ass, like yours. You didn't shy away from it in the stable."

"You took me by surprise." Something he'd been doing since they met.

At one time, she'd believed her infatuation with Detective Rossi was due to his protective caring and friendship when she'd needed both the most. But when she couldn't forget about him even though she questioned whether he was the one to betray her, she had doubts about that reasoning. Telling herself it was just lust this time around ceased working yesterday when she heard the lengths he'd gone to with arranging that picnic for her.

"If so, you've proven surprises don't stop you from taking the bull by the horns and pushing forward." Backing away from her, he rose and picked up the plates. "We'll go to Spurs this weekend, give you something else to think about besides that bastard, Cortez. I'll be installing the long countertop if you need me."

A heated rush of excitement went through Melinda without any knowledge of what to expect, her pussy swelling and dampening from imagining herself with Nick in such a place. "Houston, we have a problem," she muttered under her breath, leaning back with a sigh, eyeing his arrogant swagger with amused annoyance. How did he manage to always get in the last word, often leaving a comment dangling like that, saying just enough to keep her curious, guessing, and intrigued?

Nick swiveled his head at the door, one black brow lifted. "You talking to me? *Apollo 13*, 1995, Tom Hanks."

Nothing slipped by this man. "No, but while we're at it, *Taxi Driver*, 1976, Robert Di Niro."

"Good catch, darlin', but I'm determined to stump you one of these times."

Nick went inside, and Melinda sat there wondering if she'd made a big mistake by coming here or the smartest move since witnessing her father's murder. Either way put her future, even her life on the line.

Chapter Eight

Nick returned from his appointments by early afternoon and was somehow not surprised to spot Melinda at the fence talking to Merry, his head filling with fantasies eyeing the way her snug jeans hugged her ass. The distrustful mare stood several feet away from her but didn't appear aggressive, or even wary. He stood by his truck for a moment to observe the two, thinking they were good for each other, each still recovering from a trauma and cautious of trusting the wrong person.

The picnic surprise had gone a long way in earning Melinda's trust back, at least enough to get her to stay here. He should question why that pleased him so much, far beyond the relief of ensuring the safety of a woman whom he felt a responsibility for. The truth was, Melinda had never been far from his mind since Cheyenne, regardless of the time, distance, and silence separating them. Those weeks together at the safehouse, the bond they'd forged that he'd never experienced with another woman, certainly not a witness in a case, had impacted him more than he'd realized at the time. It had taken the sucker punch to his gut hearing Cortez was once again a threat to her then seeing her again to admit she had always meant more to him than a case.

Now, to convince Melinda they had something worth pursuing together other than seeing Cortez back behind bars. Nick might have succeeded in regaining her faith in his protectiveness, but breaching the wall guarding her feelings would take more time, effort, and patience. He possessed an abundance of the first two, but patience? Not so much.

Spenser came out of the stable, and Nick walked over to meet him, determined to find the self-restraint needed to wait for Melinda to admit what they had going was more than sex. "Any issues while I was gone?"

"No, all is good." Spenser nodded toward Melinda. "She helped spread fresh hay in the stalls. Even though Jose and I tried to tell her it wasn't necessary, she insisted."

"She's not one to sit around doing nothing." Thanks to Melinda, the safehouse had stayed clean, and, when those chores were done, she would work in gardens she planted in the fenced backyard. "Would you saddle Rose for her before you and Jose check on the herd?"

"Sure thing. She's a sweetie but spirited." Spenser looked over at Merry. "I'm hoping you'll keep that one."

Nick glanced at Melinda, her patience with Merry a sign she would make a good horsewoman. "I'm thinking about it, but I have to check finances and the cost of keeping another one. Meet me at the corral."

Melinda turned at his approach, a flash of pleasure crossing her face before she covered it with a neutral look. "Hey, how was work?"

"No issues at either stop. I appreciate you helping out in the stables, but don't feel like you have to work. You're my guest." He reached around and tugged on her braided hair, a teasing gesture but a hard enough yank for the scalp pinpricks to get her attention. Her eyes widened before her brows dipped in a frown.

Perfect.

"I refuse to sit around all day, and it's not nice to pull a girl's hair."

He smirked. "What's wrong, did you like it too much? Never mind," he said when her look went from confused to irritated. "Spenser is saddling your mount for our ride. Give me a minute to grab Ghost, and we'll head out."

She glanced behind him, smiling. "Oh, she's beautiful. I was hoping to ride her when I first saw her. But you're pretty, too, Merry," she told the scarred mare.

I guess I'll keep her, at least as long as Melinda is here, he mused, watching her dash around him to run a hand down Rose's sleek, charcoal-speckled neck. The mare gave her a friendly nudge, drawing a chuckle from Melinda. Nick didn't care for the twinge he experienced at the thought of her leaving again and whistled for Ghost. One day at a time, he thought, watching his stallion trot up to the fence. Today he'd concentrate on keeping her focused on him and not why she was here.

Nick kept one eye on Melinda as he saddled Ghost, admiring her ease in swinging up into the saddle while Spenser held Rose's reins. It might have been years since she'd gone trail riding with her family, but no one would know it looking at her relaxed posture astride the large mare.

Mounting Ghost, he waved to his hired hand. "Thanks, Spenser. We'll likely catch up with you later at the herd."

"Enjoy your ride, boss, ma'am." He tipped his hat to Melinda.

"Thank you. I'm sure I will," she returned, nudging Rose toward Nick.

"I guess I won't worry about you," he told her as they set out across the range. "You look good up there, darlin'."

She chuckled, flashing him an amused glance. "You can't help worrying, Nick. It's in your DNA. As annoying as it can be, I admit your protective streak was a comfort in Cheyenne."

"Not now though?"

Averting her face, she blew out a breath, her body swaying in tune with the mare's slow walk. "I'm still working out how I feel about Cortez's release forcing me into hiding, and seeing you again. This time around, I'm conflicted, whereas before, I was sure of what I wanted to do and why, and wasn't as scared as I am now." Facing him, she admitted, "I need you, and I'm grateful, but I don't want to be either. Does that make sense?"

His chest tightened at her stark confession. "Considering all of the circumstances, yes." He guided Ghost close enough for him to reach across and cup her chin. "So, how about we concentrate on how much we still want each other?"

"Use sex to keep the boogie man away?"

"No, to keep from fretting over the boogie man. I'll keep him away from you."

She laughed and pulled out of his grasp. "You're so arrogant. Why do I like that about you? Tell me about your club."

Nick let her change the subject, satisfied for now with their progress. "Spurs. We can socialize or play. I'll leave it up to you after I show you around and you're comfortable with the public displays. There are private rooms upstairs as an option. Several members come to visit with friends and enjoy watching the scenes before taking their play upstairs. You may like the hot tub out back, but if you wear a bathing suit, you'll stand out like a sore thumb." He took in her pensive expression and could almost see the wheels turning in her head as she tried to decide if any of that appealed to her enough to try.

"Relax," he drawled. "You don't have to make any decisions now, or even Friday night. Plan on going to have fun with some of your new friends, and that's all."

Melinda reined in Rose and swiveled to look at him, her face pink, her bright eyes curious. "Have you ever taken someone there just to hang out?"

"No. I've never dated a club member and never gotten serious enough about anyone I was seeing who wasn't in the lifestyle to bother interesting them in checking it out. Why?"

"Because I don't want you making concessions for me."

She kicked the mare into walking again, turning her gaze to scan their surroundings of wide-open, colorful flower-strewn fields, mountain ridges, and pine trees in various sizes, shapes, and green shades. He never tired of Idaho's views and beauty, regardless of the season, but she was raised with beaches and the ocean in her backyard and ideal weather year-round.

"Why not? Didn't you make major concessions in your life to look up your father then agree to testify against his killer, and even now, coming to an area so vastly different from home to fend for yourself until Cortez is back in prison?"

She huffed a laugh, flicking him an amused glance. "You make me sound like either a martyr or wonder woman. Trust me, I'm neither."

Maybe not, but he still admired the hell out of her. "Back to the subject of going to Spurs." He pointed toward a thick cluster of trees. "Follow me over there and, when we return to the ranch, you can think about whether we're going to Spurs so you can relax, have fun, and socialize, or you wish to explore the other options."

There was no mistaking the flash of curiosity in Melinda's eyes, or the fact she didn't hesitate to nod, not even to take a second to think about what he might do in those trees. Her interest in the lifestyle was already there, but Nick would have to prove that to her, a task he didn't mind in the least.

Melinda tried and failed to calm her racing heart, her pulse pounding with the heated blood rushing through her veins from imagining what Nick planned to do to her. There was no fear, no distrust, no worry, just plain, old-fashioned lust, which was easy to deal with. The emotional roller coaster she'd been riding since seeing him again was another matter, one she didn't care to delve into right now.

They dismounted at the edge of the woods, and she followed Nick's lead, tethering Rose to a low-hanging branch, leaving enough slack for the mare to bend down and graze. He joined her, checking her tying abilities then holding out a hand. It was when she glanced down to clasp his hand she noticed the coiled rope at his waist, and her throat went dry.

What did I agree to?

Granted, her previous sexual experiences were nothing to brag about, and she wouldn't label any of them adventurous, but she wasn't a timid, inexperienced, green girl, either. Okay, maybe she was when it came to kinky, she admitted when he tugged her behind him with a tight hold around her trembling fingers and sweaty palm.

"Relax, Melinda," he instructed in a firm voice, as if that would work to calm her jitters.

She opened her mouth to disabuse him of that notion then clamped it shut again as she followed him into the forest's cooler interior, realizing the nervous twitches were almost gone. By the time he halted in front of a wide, towering pine, all that remained of the uncertainty from seeing that rope was her jumping pulse. Riding next to Nick and listening to his deep timbre were responsible for her damp panties.

"This is a good option." He turned to look at her, nudging his hat back and eying her up and down before nodding. "Better. Leave your mind open to possibilities and remember the word red. Say it, and I'll stop. Say anything else, and I may not, so don't forget."

He dropped her hand, and a chill went through her from losing his warm, comforting hold. "Now I'm nervous again."

"Don't be. You're always safe with me," he stated, turning back around.

"You and the other detectives told me the same thing a year and a half ago," she reminded him, her heart twisting when he whipped around with a tortured glare.

"And all four of us paid a hefty price for that error. I've learned from our mistake. You can believe that if nothing else. Come here."

Her gaze skittered around the forest. "What do you have in mind?"

"A bondage test." Nick uncoiled the rope at his side and tossed it over a sturdy branch then pulled until both ends dangled down evenly.

She couldn't refuse him even if she wanted to, which she didn't. Nick picked up one end of the rope, and she watched, impressed as he fashioned a loop with an intricate twist and slipped it around his wrist.

"This is how easy you can free yourself." With a yank, the loop fell open then he pointed toward the trees where she could see patches of a field through the gaps. "The guys are checking my herd over there, within calling distance. You can hike over there to see for yourself. I'll wait."

The offer alone eased her mind, and she shook her head. "That's not necessary, but thanks."

"You're welcome. Ready to try this?" He held up one looped end.

Nick wasn't giving her time to balk or question or to get nervous, which she appreciated as much as his reassuring disclosure of his cowhands' whereabouts. Melinda put her hand in the reformed loop, her breath snagging as her arm lifted when he pulled down on the other side. He didn't pause before attaching her other wrist, which entailed lifting both arms up until she stood stretched under the heavy tree limb. Trailing his fingers down her arms, his rough skin left the sensitive area tingling and raised goose bumps as his dark eyes scanned her face. The last of Melinda's misgivings fell away under his intense regard.

"I'm good," she told him, willing to see where this would lead. "Red if I want you to stop, a yank to free myself."

He traced one finger down her damaged cheek. "Good girl."

The simple caress and praise produced a warm coil in her abdomen, but when that hand dropped to start undoing the buttons on her sleeveless summer blouse, she shivered. Outdoor nakedness was something else she'd never risked before today. That she was willing to do so now, with Nick in control, spoke volumes about how fast he'd eroded her trust issues.

"You're thinking too hard again. Relax, darlin'."

Damn it, Melinda couldn't think straight when Nick touched her, let alone when he drawled that endearment in his gravelly voice. She inhaled his strong, masculine scent, took in his whisker-shadowed jawline, chiseled lips, and deep brown gaze from under his Stetson. *And you're too damn sexy and appealing for my peace of mind.* "I'll try, but I've never done anything like this."

Nick flicked open her bra, and the lacy cups fell apart, baring her breasts to the soft wisp of fresh air. "Then you've been dating the wrong men." He circled a pouting nipple, tweaking the nub into a puckered, throbbing but pleasant ache.

"We're not dating," Melinda felt compelled to point out, enjoying the light breeze caressing her naked breasts with the soft strokes of a paintbrush.

"Call it what you want or deny what we have going, it doesn't matter. It is what it is." Wrapping his large hand around her breast, he pressed his fingers into the full flesh and pierced her with a direct stare. "Neither will change the fact there's been something special brewing between us since we first met. Something that's more than either of us bargained for." He kneaded her breast and dropped his other hand to her waist, opening her jeans and sliding the zipper down, never taking his eyes off her face.

Melinda sucked in a breath, his calloused fingertips scratching her skin as he slid his hand inside her loosened pants and pushed them down to her thighs, stalling her denial. From the first, this rugged cowboy had struck a chord inside her, and during those weeks of isolation had strummed it into an erotic melody of fantasy she'd wanted to play over and over. Not even her fear he was the one who had betrayed her had kept her away from him for long after her body welcomed seeing him again with a burning lust.

But all of that was physical, nothing else. He might think it could lead to something deeper and meaningful, but she would never know if guilt played a factor in his feelings.

"She traveled across the country just to get a glimpse at a man after hearing his sad story on the radio about losing his wife," Nick said, sliding a finger inside her and pressing the rough heel of his hand against her pubis.

Melinda gasped, confused by his remark while sensation blossomed between her legs. "What are you talking about?" she muttered, wanting to concentrate on the pleasure sweeping through her.

"Since you're intent on thinking about other things besides me and what I want from you, I thought we'd play our game. Which movie?"

He pulled out of her, and she whimpered, already so needy she couldn't bear to lose his touch. She jerked her hips forward, griping, "I don't want to play games, Nick. Damn it, I want..." She stopped short of saying she wanted him, not ready to give him that much control over her.

"If you can't admit it, trust me enough to show you," he bit out in a hardened tone before delving into his jeans pocket.

That firm voice worked every time, and, when he held up a purple silicone U-shaped toy, she flushed with hot expectancy. "Is that a vibrator?"

He turned the narrowest side toward her. "A clit stimulator, and this"—he flipped it around—"will pulse against your G-spot. I'll show you."

Melinda couldn't believe she was so willing and eager to try the toy out here, but she nodded, waiting with bated breath as he slowly worked the slimmer piece inside her pussy, leaving the wider side snug against the apex of her spread labia. Her pelvis jerked from the erotic pressure, a light sheen of perspiration covering her body as soon as he turned it on. *"Oh!"* she breathed, dropping her head back and closing her eyes as small vibrations beat against sensitive tissue.

Nick's chuckle resounded in her ear, his lips tugging sharply on her earlobe, those large hands closing around her breasts. "Like that, do you? I can't wait to demonstrate the higher pulsations and its other uses. But not yet. I want to play with you first."

The pleasurable pulses between her legs distracted her from his comments but not his hands. Keeping her eyes closed, she relished the slow sweep of his palms down her sides, around her back, and over her clenching buttocks. He teased her to the point of frustration, running his fingers all over her butt and between her cheeks. With a pinch of discomfort, he breached her tight rear orifice, her eyes flying open with the sudden sparks adding heat to the already hot spasms erupting inside her pussy.

Embarrassed by how much she liked the slow, shallow dips inside this new-to-her erogenous zone, she moaned in uncertainty at her sudden wish for a deeper, harder pressure. As if reading her thoughts, he covered her lips with his, his kiss accompanying a surge in the vibrations against her clit and G-spot. Her already simmering arousal heated into harder contractions around the vibrator, and Melinda shook, grateful for the restraints holding her up and Nick's muscled strength to lean against.

He held her mouth captive for endless seconds while she adjusted to the more intense sensations spreading through her lower body, both from the vibrations and deeper, hard plunges inside her rectum. By the time he lifted his head, he'd reduced her to a mass of quivering neediness and on the verge of begging. She flushed as he pinned her pelvis against the rough denim and thick bulge behind his zipper, using his thumb in her butt to hold her there and showing her the remote in his other hand.

"Enjoy, darlin'."

By enjoy, she discovered he meant take more of what the vibrator offered, including the faster, harder pulsations against those tender nerve endings. The direct, forceful pounding assaulted already inflamed tissues, and her pussy spasmed in response, quick, tight clutches of her inner muscles around the embedded clit stimulator. She quivered in the bonds, now grateful for the restraints that left her no choice but to accept the bombardment of new sensations. She shoved the option to say red aside, already past the point of no return in accepting this decadent outdoor ecstasy.

"Nick." Melinda moaned, closing her eyes again as he slowed the pulses and dipped his head, wrapping his lips around one aching nipple. Arching her torso forward, she begged in silence for more, unable to voice the desperation taking over her body for a return of those stronger vibrations.

Nick drew on her tip, pulling up, elongating her nipple using his teeth, the sharp pinpricks skydiving straight down to her toes. "You don't need to say anything. I know what you want, what you need," he stated with confidence once he released her nipple.

He switched from that throbbing, tortured nub to the other side, clamping down on that nipple with as much voracious hunger as its twin before leaving off both to remove his thumb and shuffle behind her. Melinda writhed in frustration, her entire body ablaze with spiraling arousal, the gripping pleasure on the precipice of consuming her. His arm came around her waist, his rippling muscles hard against her soft abdomen, his splayed hand on her side a welcome hold. Without warning, his arm tightened, and his other hand descended in a blistering spank covering one buttock. Her cheek bounced from the blow, hot pleasure/ pain spreading over her flesh. He shocked her further by upping the vibrations again and then continued swatting her in tune to the hard pulse.

Her climax hovered while he numbed her buttocks with his hard hand, her breathing growing labored under the dual, contradicting assault on her body until she erupted from the torment.

Melinda's startled cry echoed in the woods, turning into a series of mewling whimpers as he continued to slap her backside with a steady barrage of smacks.

Her pussy released a spate of abundant cream, squeezing the small dildo with tight, convulsive clutches, leaving her to wallow in the euphoria for endless moments, mindless of her surroundings until awareness returned in slow degrees. By the time the fog cleared from her head, Nick was removing the clit teaser and reaching for her bound hands. She fell against him as soon as her arms dropped, grateful for his strong support when his arms wrapped around her.

Sighing against his neck, Melinda let her body settle while she got a grip on her intense emotions. She wasn't positive she could have handled such a powerful orgasm without Nick making sure she'd felt his hands on her the whole time, his whispered assurances close to her ear.

He continued touching her, assuaging her throbbing, hot buttocks with light caresses, her heart rolling over with his praise. "You were wonderful, Melinda, taking everything I dished out, gifting me with your climax."

A giggle burst through her trembling lips, and she shifted to gaze up at him. "I should thank you, and I will when I'm able to think clearly and wrap my mind around what just occurred." She shook her head against his chest. Her hot throbbing buttocks, along with the continued ripples traveling up and down her sheath, kept her bemused over how she ended up in this state.

"You trusted me enough to let go, that's what happened." He pulled her jeans up and fastened her bra, leaning back enough for her to see his face. "When you're ready, we'll ride to the lake and water the horses before returning to the ranch."

I can get used to this.

That thought brought her up short. Until today, she hadn't believed there was anything between them except a physical attraction that had sprung from her need for protection and his job to provide it, regardless of Nick's assertions there was something more. She couldn't imagine allowing any other man to bind her like that, allowing unfettered access to her body to do with as he pleased. She'd never begged a man for anything until him, either, and wasn't prepared to lose yet more of herself until she could do so without a serious threat to her life hanging in the balance.

Her muscles still trembled, but otherwise, Melinda was as good as she would get, preferring to collect the rest of her thoughts in private. "No more babying," she stated, buttoning her top. She found the steady beat of his heart and his strong arms soothing balms against her current emotional upheaval, something else she could get used to if she wasn't careful. "As you can see, I didn't fall apart or come undone."

"No, you never do, do you? Come along, then."

Nick was confident he'd broken through another barrier keeping Melinda from giving him her complete trust, but she still refused to engage her full emotions. The physical submission was coming easy for her, not so the emotional. For the first time ever, he was as interested in gaining a woman's affections as her physical responses. He boosted her into the saddle, watching her face for signs of discomfort, but she was good at putting on a bland expression to mask her inner turmoil.

He mounted Ghost and veered toward

the lake, a shimmer of glassy blue at this distance. Melinda edged over next to him, her tempting lips curled in a teasing grin. *"Sleepless in Seattle."*

It took a minute for that to register then he returned her smile. "Took you long enough to figure out what movie I was talking about."

"You were distracting me earlier."

"And yet your mind kept wandering to other things." When she remained silent, he prodded, "No answer, huh?"

"Nope."

Nick dropped it, deeming it best to let her work her way through her feelings for him in her own way and time. He was just now coming to terms with how deeply he cared for Melinda, and he wasn't betrayed nearly to the extent she was. Riding back to the ranch, he hoped there were no more surprises for her to deal with, and to help ensure that, he would make certain his former boss still had eyes on Cortez.

****

One down, two to go.

Cortez jumped into the car his contact had left for him one street over from his house last night and drove away from Owen Philips' house with no one the wiser. He chuckled, recalling the detective's startled expression when he'd awoken to struggle with Cortez's weight pinning him down. Between his bum leg, extra weight, and age, it had taken little effort for Cortez to shove the sleeping pills down his throat. He left the little prick drifting into a permanent sleep he wouldn't wake from.

The night was going so well, he was tempted to visit his favorite bar before sneaking back into his house but wouldn't push his luck. According to his lawyer, the cops would be called off sometime tomorrow, leaving him free to go about his business. Tonight, unaware he'd slipped out, they were the perfect alibi. After seeing to a few more details, he would drive to Idaho and finish the two loose ends there before taking off for Canada. He wasn't sticking around to go to prison for killing cops and didn't doubt they would come for him as the number one suspect after he offed the girl and Rossi.

Life might have been much easier before he'd killed Theo, but anticipation hummed through his veins as he thought about the two other bodies he would leave behind before relocating. Who said revenge wasn't sweet?

Chapter Nine

"Why did you quit your job in Cheyenne?"

The moon's bright glow was the only light source beaming in through Nick's window, casting a bluish splash across the bed where Melinda lay spooned in front of him. His thick arm muscles rippled under her stroking hand, the comfort of his hold not lost on her, just ignored for now.

"I hope it wasn't because of me, and my refusal to testify after that night." She didn't want to be the cause of him giving up a career he'd obviously loved, one he'd been good at for almost fifteen years if she remembered correctly.

"Sorry, but yes, you, what happened to you, and the betrayal by someone I was close to and trusted all factored in on my decision. If it makes you feel better, I was ready for a change before your case came up. I spent that first six months after you returned home investigating the leak and gave up when I completed a farrier course."

Melinda forced herself to stay focused on his words and not let the deep rumble of his voice in her ear and his heavy arm and thighs distract her, an almost impossible task. Her butt rested against his semierect cock, another distraction even though the way they'd torn up the sheets less than an hour ago had left her wrung out. She was turning into quite a hussy, lusting after him and always wanting more.

"You mentioned owning a horse back then. Was that Ghost?"

"Yes. I bought Rose after you left. I wanted more for them than the stable where I boarded them."

She turned her head around and rammed his chin. "Sorry. Will Merry ever be ridable?"

Lowering his head, he nipped her neck, a sharp prick that stole her breath, a reaction she experienced every time he put his mouth or hands on her.

"Odds are, she won't ever let someone on

her. I planned to relocate her to a sanctuary, but I may not."

Melinda's heart ached for the victimized horse. "I hope you don't. She's a sweetie, and she's been through enough changes."

His chest vibrated against her back with his deep chuckle. "Only you would call that horse sweet, but then, only you would threaten to shoot me for trying to help you."

"And yet, here I am, for now anyway." The thought of returning home and never seeing him again saddened her as much as when she'd left Cheyenne.

"Yes, for now," he murmured. "Go to sleep, Melinda."

"Okay." She was more than happy to set aside plaguing thoughts for much-needed sleep.

A few days later, Melinda sat perched on the top fence rail watching Nick working a new horse, the midmorning sun warm on her shoulders and the only sounds those of Mother Nature. She was trying to think of a pastime she enjoyed back home as much as she did eyeballing Nick astride a horse with the pine-covered mountain ridges behind him. The flash of his white teeth in his tanned face when his mount obeyed a command without flaw revealed his boyish pleasure and enthusiasm for his work. He alternated gaits, running then slowing while tugging the reins left then right, his forearms rippling as he steered the horse in different directions.

This was so different than how she'd spent her time off back home. She supposed she would eventually miss bike riding down to the beach to meet friends or hanging out until two a.m. at her favorite club. Odds were, the absence of constant busy traffic and dealing with hordes of people wherever she went would get to her by the time she returned home, the relative peaceful quiet and the vast openness home to more wildlife than people having turned boring. Melinda thought of Mr. Fairfax and wondered if he'd passed away, wishing she could have stayed and seen his case through to the end. She had arrived in Idaho two and a half weeks ago and missed working but admitted Nick was making it easier for her to stick around. Thus far, she liked the differences in locale and getting reacquainted with Nick now that she trusted him enough to let her guard down.

Melinda should have realized she was fighting a losing battle from the moment he found her at the cabin. He'd given her the same enigmatic look of concern and admiration as when he'd introduced himself for the first time. A shudder went through her remembering the traumatizing events that had landed her at the police station. Recounting what she'd seen to the cream-your-panties cowboy cop hadn't been easy.

"Ms. Walsh, I'm Detective Rossi."

Melinda's legs were still too shaky to try and stand, but she held out her hand, the warm, snug clasp of his grip easing her tremors. "Melinda, please."

The small private room where she'd been led after telling the desk cop she'd witnessed a murder suddenly seemed smaller as the tall, broad-shouldered detective took a seat across from her at the table. He handed her the soda she hadn't noticed clutched in his other hand.

"Melinda, you look like you could use this."

His deep voice washed through her, and, when he removed his Stetson, revealing his laser-sharp, concerned brown gaze, her racing heart calmed. "Since I doubt you have a bottle of whiskey sitting around, this will do. Thank you." She swallowed a drink of the cold caffeine, but it was his calm, steady gaze that enabled her to repeat her story.

"Take your time, Melinda, and tell me what brought you here. I promise, you're safe."

Melinda sucked in a deep breath as Nick took his attention off the horse long enough to check on her. He would do the same thing at the safehouse, wherever she was or whatever she was doing, keeping a close eye on how she was faring under the pressure of being cooped up for so long. She had insisted her feelings for the protective detective stemmed from appreciation for the extra effort he put into keeping her mind off the upcoming trial. He made the long days fun with their movie trivia bantering, always arriving with a DVD, insisting he would find one she hadn't seen. He never did, and she enjoyed ribbing him as they would watch it together.

The lustful fantasies she wove involving him helped her through the nights, so much so, she would wake up damp, aching for him to distract her from worry with his hard body. The reality of what she was doing had hit her hard that last night, and he was there for her again, knowing what she needed more than she.

How could she not fall in love with him?

Melinda blew out a breath, shaking her head at her own stupidity. What had made her believe she could keep from falling for him all over again even though she could no longer trust him? He kept insisting there was more between them than cop and witness, but the pain of betrayal was difficult to get over. She might not believe he'd been the one who had sold her out, but either Captain Honeycutt or one of the three detectives assigned to her protection had slipped up in front of the mole. Without those answers, she would be unable to look in the mirror without reliving the horror of that night.

She started to hop down off the fence when Nick trotted toward the corral but saw Merry approaching on her own. Melinda's heart rolled over, pleasure swamping her as the recalcitrant mare stopped a few feet away and pawed at the ground. Melinda had taken to tossing her an apple or carrot when she visited Merry in the stable, saying, "Here's your treat," but the mare had kept her distance from her as well as everyone else while out in the pasture.

"Hello, sweetie. Are you looking for your treat?" Merry's ears perked up, and Melinda realized she recognized the word treat. She pulled from her pocket the two carrots she'd picked up on the way out in case one of the horses approached her. "Lucky for you, I have these..." She paused, her mouth going dry and her throat constricting as Merry slowly came right up to her. "Oh God, please don't take my hand off." Holding the carrot by the very end, she prepared to snatch her hand back, but Merry took the other end nicely and chewed, her soft eyes never wavering from Melinda's face.

Tears pricked Melinda's eyes, and she ached to stroke Merry's nose but wouldn't push her luck. She choked on a watery laugh when the mare whinnied and tossed her head at the other carrot. "Okay, okay. Here you go." This time, she trotted off with the carrot, done with her now that she'd gotten her treat.

"Congratulations, darlin', you've managed to accomplish in less than a week what I couldn't in the last month."

Melinda barely had time to grab Nick's shoulders before he lifted her off the fence, his hands gripping her waist. His uneasy expression was at odds with his lighthearted tone, a familiar combo from before but not one she'd seen since they'd met again. "She took me by surprise when she came to me." She inhaled his masculine scent, suppressing the urge to lick the bead of sweat rolling down his neck. With her nose a breath away from the curly black hairs exposed by his unbuttoned shirt, it was easier to run her lips and teeth over that exposed skin.

"Keep that up and you'll risk Spenser and Jose seeing more of you than you might like," he warned.

Her pussy dampened, her nipples going hard, his comment firing up her imagination along with her senses, and she groaned.

"What have you done to me, Nick?"

"Nothing you weren't ripe for and willing to try." His jaw went rigid seconds before his phone beeped. Dropping his hands from her hips, he checked the caller ID and scowled. "This isn't good," he said before answering. "Captain."

Nick's terse greeting to his former boss sent a chill of foreboding down Melinda's spine. "When?" he snapped, pinning her with a dark stare as he said, "I'm not saying. Just keep me posted."

Melinda wasted no time asking, "What aren't you saying? What's happened?"

"Owen Phillips tried to commit suicide and is in a coma, critical, and Honeycutt was forced to take the cops off Cortez. When he went by his place after they left, he wasn't there. He's not sure if Cortez is still in town and doesn't have just cause to track him down. Honeycutt wanted to know where we are."

"You don't trust him? That's why you left Cheyenne without telling anyone where you were moving?"

"I wouldn't trust Mike with your life if

he were alive, and he was like a brother to me. Fuck, what was Owen thinking?" Regret laced his rough voice.

"I'm so sorry about Detective Philips." Of the three detectives, he was the oldest and more by the book than Nick or Mike, friendly but not chummy the way the other two were.

"Me, too. I didn't stay in touch with him once he retired, which I should have. He'd already been struggling with depression after his wife left." He released a sigh, saying, "Water under the bridge now. Give me time to shower, and I'll drive you into town for your lunch with the girls. Until I'm sure Cortez isn't anywhere around these parts, I don't want you going anywhere alone."

Melinda bristled at his implacable tone but bit her lip against arguing when she saw the raw grief in his dark eyes. She might not like his high-handedness but understood the motivation behind his attitude. That didn't stop her from putting in her two cents.

"Fine, but get lost after you drop me at the deli. I'll call you when we're done. *If* Cortez managed to track me here, he won't try anything in public." At least, she didn't think he would jeopardize his recent luck in getting out of a twenty-year prison sentence by doing something stupid.

"Agreed."

A calculating look came over his face, and he reached behind her to cradle her nape in his large hand. Tightening his hold, he brought her up on her toes until her breasts pressed against his chest and his mouth hovered above her lips. Melinda's pulse spiked, and she clutched his upper arms to anchor herself against his potency.

"One thing. Do not dictate to me like that when we go to Spurs tomorrow night. I'd hate to punish you in public your first night."

He kissed her, stalling Melinda's reply with the slow, soft glide of his lips over hers, his tongue stroking hers as if he couldn't get enough of her taste. When he released her, she couldn't decide if she wanted to smack him because of her heated reaction to that threat or jump him for the same reason.

"I'm pretty open-minded, or thought I was since what you've told me until now sounded intriguing, but you'll have to explain that issue in more detail before we get there."

"Relax." Nick wrapped an arm around her shoulders and headed toward the house. "Just like here, you can stop anything with one word."

Yes, but how disappointed will you be if I can't get into the lifestyle that is so much a part of you? Melinda hadn't considered that, and now she was even more hesitant to let herself think they could make something of their relationship.

****

Finally, something was going his way, Cortez thought, excitement pumping up his spirits at seeing Melinda Walsh with Rossi. He waited for another car to pass in front of him before leaving his hidden spot behind a cluster of trees and turning onto the main road to follow Rossi's truck. He hadn't wasted any time leaving Cheyenne, still fuming over his failure to take out Phillips.

When he'd read in the paper the detective was in a coma following a suicide attempt, he'd cursed his bad luck but didn't worry overmuch. From all accounts, the doctors didn't expect the bastard to recover. Maybe a slow death hooked up to machines was more fitting. After spending all day yesterday searching for the cabin Barry gave him directions to only to discover a family of four now occupied the place, his patience had come to an end. By this time, his temper was a hair trigger away from exploding.

Locating Rossi's ranch this morning had been much easier, and the long hours he'd spent sitting there waiting for a chance to confirm Rossi was there had just paid off in spades. He'd thought finding them together would be too much to hope for, but his luck had finally changed course. He tailed them with one car separating him from the truck until they reached a small town. Instead of risking exposure without a clear plan, he pulled into a gas station and started back to the motel just outside of Boise to figure out his next step.

****

"Wait, and I'll walk you in," Nick stated when Melinda reached for the door handle as soon as he parked in front of the deli.

"For pity's sake, Nick," she returned, flashing him a look of exasperation. "What's going to happen to me out in the open, on a busy street? It's three steps into the deli."

"Humor me."

He got out, the prickles he always experienced before something bad happened still plaguing him. They'd started on and off yesterday only to increase today, the persistent odd sensation putting him on edge. Did he think Cortez would act so rashly out in public? No, but during his interrogation of the lowlife drug dealer, Cortez didn't bother hiding his hatred of their eyewitness or muffling his threats, ignoring his attorney's advice when he told Cortez to keep his mouth shut and temper under control. Nick wouldn't put anything past Cortez and wouldn't gamble with Melinda's life.

"There's nothing funny about this," she grumbled as he searched up and down the street, holding the door open.

"No, there's not. But thank you for cooperating. With all the tourists visiting town, Cortez or anyone he hired could blend in unnoticed until it's too late."

Melinda grimaced. "I didn't think of that."

Confident she understood the reason for his concern, he said, "That's what you have me for," then started to leave when he caught sight of Sophie sitting with Skye and Amie. "I'm glad Sophie joined you. She had a recent scare and can commiserate with what you're going through. Call me when you're done."

Nick returned to his truck and drove to the sheriff's office one street over, praying the prickles of unease that served as a bad omen stayed away. He picked up burgers and filled Shawn in on Cortez while they ate. They pulled up Cortez's mugshots, and Shawn promised to distribute copies to his deputies, Clayton, and Dakota.

"I'll shoot his photo over to Ben and Neil also," Shawn said, standing to walk out with Nick.

"The more the better. The rangers can scout the campgrounds, something I should have considered." He needed to do better if he planned to keep Melinda safe.

"Don't beat yourself up over little things.

Come out to the club tomorrow night and take her mind off worrying."

Nick slid behind the wheel with a nod of appreciation. Shawn and the other men had filled the void left by Mike's death and leaving the department, despite his resolve to remain detached. Without their unquestioning support, he'd likely risk Melinda running from him again by trying to keep her holed up inside his house where he could be sure she stayed safe. He wished he could talk her into testifying again, but her trust extended only so far and wouldn't go beyond him. And that was only because he'd jumped through hoops to get where they were now. Hell, he didn't blame her though. He would do the same in her place.

Nick started the truck then leaned his arm on the open window. "That's my plan. It'll be the first time I've taken on a newbie. Should be interesting for both of us."

"And entertaining." Shawn nodded. "See you tomorrow."

It was after midnight when Nick woke from a sound sleep next to Melinda, cursing the return of prickling unease crawling under his skin. If he weren't so sure the strange vibes plaguing him were meant to alert him in some way, he would ignore them in favor of staying wrapped around her warm, bare body. Instead, he crawled out of bed, slipped on his jeans, and padded out onto the front porch. It took a moment for his eyes to adjust to the darkness, but when he did, he wasn't able to see anything out of the ordinary. Yet his uneasiness remained, propelling him down to the stables.

He smelled gasoline before he reached the building and a quick search of the perimeter revealed small flames already licking up the south side. Dashing inside, he hit the alarm to rouse Spenser and Jose from the loft then flung open the rear door before releasing the horses that were already panicking. Within seconds, Spenser and Jose were outside, grabbing the hoses attached to the well and soaking the stable wall. Nick was still working at breathing past the panic when he saw Melinda running toward him. Suspecting Cortez was behind the arson, the dread returned, and, with it, a surge of anger at her disregard for her safety.

"My, God, Nick, what happened?" she gasped, her eyes darting from the flames toward the pitch-black pasture as if searching for the horses' safety.

Through the roaring in his head, Nick barely registered the fact she wore the T-shirt he'd tossed on the bedroom chair and was barefoot. Clasping her arm, he insisted, "This could have been Cortez. Get back to the house."

Melinda got that closed, stubborn look on her face and jerked out of his hold. "I'm helping, and we don't have time to waste arguing."

Swearing, he handed her a hose. "Then start spraying."

It took them over an hour before Nick announced the rest of the stable was safe from harm. The volunteer fire department couldn't do anything else, and law enforcement wouldn't find anything in the dark they hadn't already seen, but highway patrol could keep an eye on his property tonight. He made a quick call to Shawn who promised to get someone out there tonight and be here first thing in the morning.

Nick hung up, feeling better, then beckoned to Spenser and Jose. "The sheriff is sending someone tonight to keep an eye on the property and will help assess the damage tomorrow. The stable is safe for you to go back to bed. Thanks." He didn't wait to hear their reply, jerking on Melinda's arm to haul her inside the house before turning on her. "What were you thinking?" he snapped, slamming the door. "You know there's a damn good chance Cortez is looking for you, and, as soon as there's trouble, you make yourself a target. Do I have to lock you up in a safehouse again?"

"Because I was so safe last time?" she shot back, jerking out of his hold and moving away. "Excuse me for being concerned about you."

"I can live without your concern, but I can't survive being responsible for you getting hurt again." With his heart still slamming against his rib cage, he took her shoulders and pinned her against the wall, the smell of burned wood still assailing his nostrils, reminding him what almost happened.

"Fuck, Melinda, I couldn't take it if you were hurt again on my watch, let alone killed."

The instant wave of panicked fear that had consumed Nick upon realizing the potential danger she was in tonight revealed how deep his feelings were for Melinda. When she'd refused to see him in the hospital following her attack and then returned home wanting nothing more to do with the case or him, she'd left him no choice but to let her go. This time around, he planned on getting under her skin deep enough she would have no choice but to accept what they had together.

"I'm sorry. I didn't think, just reacted when I saw the smoke. But damn it, Nick, this is my battle, too. I *need* to be in on the fight."

He heard the catch in her voice and eased up on his anger and his grip, once again striving for calm through a deep breath. His cock strained against his zipper, engorged with the primitive urge to bind her to him with sex, drive into her over and over until he'd staked his claim. So strong was the need pounding through his veins, he slid a hand under the T-shirt and yanked down the loose gym shorts.

Going to one knee, he buried his face between her quivering thighs and growled against her puffy labia, "Then think about this, and nothing else. That I can accept."

Using his thumbs, he spread her folds and speared her damp flesh with his tongue, her soft mewls music to his ears, the prick of her nails gripping his shoulders a sharp pain he relished. He dove deep, stroking her slick muscles then wrapping around her swollen clit. Nick circled the small bud, sliding his hands behind her to palm her ass. Kneading the taut muscles, he drew on her clit with his lips, suckling until a gush of abundant cream filled his mouth and a strident cry spilled from her lips.

"Nick!"

Satisfied, he released her flesh and stood, intent on taking her further than she'd ever gone with anyone else. Clasping her hand, he tugged her over to the sofa and bent her over. Standing behind her upturned, bared ass, he released his cock and leaned over her back, nestling his erection between her buttocks.

"I want you here." He drew down then up, liking how her cheeks clenched alongside his gliding shaft. "I need to take you here." Shifting his hips, he dipped inside her pussy over and over, her low moans and gyrating hips egging him on until he returned to her tempting back hole and pushed his damp cockhead against the puckered entrance.

"I've never..." She moaned as he squeezed past her tight resistance, her juices easing his way. "Oh," she breathed softly, squirming her hips to either dislodge him or adjust to the feel of his crown breaching such a tight, unexpected orifice.

"I'll take that." Easing upward, he held her hips and pulled out of her then tunneled back inside a little easier. Once more, he pulled out and worked past her sphincter to embed his cockhead inside the hot confines of her dark channel, careful not to go too fast or too deep.

"That will have to do for now," he rasped, pulling out of her ass and digging a condom out of his pocket. Nick sheathed his glistening cock, the tension riding him so hard the last twenty minutes finally abating as he tunneled through her parted, welcoming pussy lips.

Melinda's breath released on a *swoosh* and a shudder, the discomfort from her first try at anal penetration gone, replaced with rippling pleasure as Nick filled her aching, empty pussy. His shaken reaction to the possible danger she'd inadvertently placed herself in had been as contagious as his lust. Right now, assuaging the raw need consuming her, though, was her first priority. But soon she would have to decide what was more important, protecting herself against heartache or risking that pain by taking the chance on Nick she'd denied them both for so long.

Nick slammed his groin against hers, his tight hold on her hips the only thing keeping her in place. The blood rushed to her head hanging between her braced arms as she took every plunging stroke with escalating pleasure. Her senses engaged in his rough possession: her skin perspiring, breath catching, eyes swimming, and her nose filling with the scent of their bodies' release. She cried out with her climax, her muscles clamping around his pistoning dick, her copious juices easing the way for his thickness as he pummeled her depths harder and then quickened with his orgasm. His guttural groan spurred her on, and, when he released one hip to root out her clit to press the tender piece of flesh against the unyielding ridges of his cock, she exploded again.

Melinda's brain blurred from the blend of smaller climax-abating contractions with the strong burst of new ones. She remained so awash in euphoria, she didn't notice Nick pulling out of her clutching vagina until he was helping her upright and lifting her in his arms.

"Relax now, darlin'. Cortez would be an idiot to strike again tonight," he said, tucking her back in bed then joining her. "We'll figure this out tomorrow."

She wondered if he meant their relationship or the fire that could or could not have been Cortez.

Chapter Ten

Cortez barely made it back to his car unseen after spotting Rossi come out of his house. Between the detective's focus on the stable and the inky darkness of night cloaking the field between the building and his hidey niche, he'd escaped unnoticed. This time. What the hell had awakened Rossi? Cortez had been so quiet, not even the two hired hands sleeping upstairs had roused. Rossi's sudden appearance had screwed his plan to reach the trees and pick Rossi and the girl off when the flames engulfing the stable roused them and they rushed outside. They would have been so intent on saving the horses and his men, they would never know what hit them.

His frustration knew no bounds as he returned to the motel, contemplating his options. He didn't doubt his spot behind those trees was now compromised. The first thing Rossi would do was search for clues, and that would include how the culprit – him – could get away so fast. He decided he would have to choose between giving up and heading out to Canada now or trying one more time to free himself of Walsh's testimony.

Cortez hated losing, and he wouldn't run away in defeat.

****

Melinda was on the phone to her mother when Nick got out of the shower the next morning. She wore his T-shirt again, only when she reached into an upper cabinet for plates, he saw she wasn't wearing the gym shorts, just her silk panties. Her buttocks clenched, and he recalled the pleasure of those soft cheeks in his hands, the tight grip of her ass around his cockhead. She had taken everything he'd given her last night without much hesitation, another gift of her trust she likely didn't realize she'd given.

The coffee was on, and she'd managed

to find his waffle maker. The threat last night must not have shaken her, for which he was glad. If nothing else, the fierce glint in her bright-blue eyes when she turned her megawatt gaze on him hinted she was as ready to take on Cortez now as she'd been following her father's murder, before someone had betrayed them both.

"If Cortez is responsible for almost hurting those horses, he picked the wrong way to try and scare me. Breakfast is ready."

Is it any wonder I fell in love almost from the first?

Nick kept that to himself for now. "And I'm starving. Thank you." He joined her at the table, risking an argument when he stated bluntly, "Can I count on you to stay inside until Shawn comes out and I file a report?"

"I have to stay safe to see he pays, don't I?" she returned in a frosty tone. "I don't want to, I don't like it, but I'm not stupid. But if you don't give me something to do, I'll take my irritation out on you."

"You're in a mood this morning." He wasn't sure what mood that was, but since first meeting her, he'd seen her fierce determination to take down Cortez and acceptance of the necessary sacrifices she would have to make to ensure that happened. "You still have the choice of testifying."

"No way, not until you find out who is working with Cortez."

Nick couldn't blame her. Her scars were a constant reminder of the physical torment Cortez had put her through. Losing Mike had hit him hard, but he couldn't imagine her emotional struggle dealing with witnessing not only her father's brutal murder but his partner's also.

"Then, if Cortez is coming after you, we have no choice but to take every precaution until we bring him down." He emphasized "we," hoping it helped her to know he planned on working with her, was not expecting her to make all the sacrifices. Setting aside his need to lock her away someplace safe would be hard to do, but it was better than her taking off again on her own. "I haven't gotten around to painting the spare bedrooms but have the paint. You interested?"

Her beaming smile spoke volumes. "I am."

Nick nodded then held up his fork holding a bite of golden waffle. "These are great. Cinnamon?"

"Yes, with a dash of nutmeg." Melinda sipped her coffee before taking her last bite then offering, "I'll clean up so you can watch for the sheriff."

"He should be here soon." Nick took time to give her a thorough kiss before he dug out the painting supplies and reminded her to lock the door when he went out to speak with Spenser and Jose. She wasn't his only responsibility. He shuddered to think what would have befallen his loyal employees had his strange sixth sense not kicked in, alerting him to potential danger.

Both Spenser and Jose were already hard at work tending to the horses who still appeared skittish this morning, Merry baring her teeth at Spenser as he approached. Nick decided Melinda would be the best one to work with her. With luck, all the progress she'd inadvertently made with the recalcitrant mare wasn't erased by last night's close call.

Jose met him at the gate, his face reflecting concern and anger. "That was bad shit last night, boss. How's the girl?"

"As pissed as we are. The sheriff will be here soon. After I get his take, I want to talk to you and Spenser. It may not be safe for you to continue staying over at night."

Jose squared his shoulders, straightening to his full five-foot-seven height. "We don't run away from trouble."

"And I appreciate the support, but you're my responsibility, therefore, it will be my call." Nick squeezed Jose's shoulder. "I have enough baggage on my conscience, Jose."

"Okay," he agreed with a reluctant nod before a sly grin creased his dark face. "There's an ideal spot to camp just beyond your property line."

Nick should threaten to fire him, but they both knew he wouldn't, so why waste his breath? Besides, that kind of loyalty was hard to come by. "If you're that determined to stick close, you may as well keep bunking in the loft. At least you'll have a bed and shelter. Keep your rifles close at all times though."

Spenser strolled over and rested his forearms on the fence, his gaze bouncing between Nick and Jose. "What's up?"

"Jose will tell you, and you can give me your two cents after I check on Ghost." Nick heard them talking and Spenser gripe "what the hell," counting himself lucky when he'd hired those two.

Merry kept her distance as he crossed the field, but she never did come up to him on her own, not even with coaxing or bribery unless he would threaten to walk away with his offering. Once he scouted around with Shawn and verified it was safe for her to come out, he would help Melinda settle Merry in the barn before leaving for the club tonight. It took thirty minutes to check on all the horses, but the timing was perfect, he mused, seeing Shawn's cruiser pulling up in front of the house. He didn't expect the other vehicles, so when Dakota and Clayton exited the police SUV followed by Ben, Neil, and Randy climbing out of the truck behind them, he sucked in a deep breath of gratitude.

"I didn't know you were bringing the cavalry," he said, his tension easing as he approached his friends. With this kind of support, Cortez would be a fool to stick around.

"It's not just our women we rally around when there's trouble. How's Melinda?" Shawn asked, glancing toward the house.

"Upset, pissed but solid." Nick's gaze swept the six men. "I appreciate this."

Dakota shrugged his big shoulders. "It's what we do. I'll start tracking."

"We'll join Dakota and spread out." Ben gave him a thumbs-up then he and Neil started out after Dakota.

Randy clapped him on the back. "Let's take a look at your stable."

Nick led the way, pointing to the ground along the side of the stable where he'd smelled the accelerant. Shawn took dirt samples while Clayton took pictures before they started removing several charred slats.

"Definitely gasoline," Shawn said, sealing his dirt samples. "You can still smell it beyond the odor of burnt wood." He turned his head toward the trees when a series of whistles pierced the air from that direction. "Dakota's found something. Let's join him. I have all I need from here."

Nick fumed as Dakota pointed out the recent tire ruts in the little-used turn-off from the main road. Peering through the gaps in the cluster of trees, he had a clear view of his property, the quarter mile between this spot and the stable a doable distance to cover in a few minutes at a sprint if someone was in good shape. Last time he'd seen Cortez, the thirty-five-year-old fitness buff could easily escape detection in the dark.

"Right under my fucking nose." That infuriated him more than anything.

Ben sent him a commiserating look. "Don't beat yourself up over what you couldn't know. I found out that doesn't help when I learned someone was after Amie. Are you sure you can't convince Melinda to testify? She seems to trust you now."

"No, she's adamant on that. Whoever betrayed her protection could still be on the force and in touch with Cortez. She won't chance that again."

"Dirty cops – they're the worst," Shawn muttered.

Neil glanced up from examining the tire tracks. "I agree, but don't blame her. She's been through a lot. We don't even know if he's in the area, let alone have any clues that hint this prank was him."

They returned to their vehicles, Randy saying, "We have the picture of Cortez you sent us. All we can do is keep an eye out for now."

"And nail the bastard to the wall if we see him," Dakota growled before folding his big frame onto the front passenger seat.

Nick liked that idea and expressed his gratitude as they prepared to leave. "Melinda's first visit to a club will take her mind off him. See you all tonight."

****

Spurs was nothing like Melinda imagined. Her pulse kicked up a notch seeing the people dancing to the low beat of music when she entered the club with Nick. Even from across the large, high-ceilinged room, she could make out the possessive hold several men retained on their partner, the slow sway of their close bodies suggestive without appearing lewd as she'd expected. A few of the tables were occupied, one younger girl appearing quite happy perched on a man's lap with her demi bra hanging open, her partner enjoying her bared breast as he conversed with another man seated with them. Melinda grew warm watching the casual way the other man reached over and tweaked the girl's other nipple, her face suffusing with color, her nipples puckering tighter as she squirmed.

"Huh," she muttered. "That is hot." Hot, yes, but again, not appearing vulgar.

Nick squeezed her hand, drawing her attention away from that table. "Never enjoyed two men's attention at the same time?"

"No, along with a lot of other things, it seems. I thought tying women up and public sex was all that went on at places like this." She swept her hand out to indicate the room. "I do see the odd contraptions I expected."

"Alternative sexual practices can range anywhere from innocent voyeurism to an intense scene of sensation play. My job is to help you discover what you need and then what you enjoy. Let's start with a drink."

The wood floor was smooth under her bare feet as they headed toward the bar,

Melinda not as uncomfortable parading around in public wearing Nick's shirt as she'd presumed. "What about what you need and enjoy?" She didn't want a one-sided relationship.

He gave her one of his long, speculative stares before answering. "I get my pleasure from yours, but thank you for caring enough to ask. I have to say, you're more relaxed than I thought you would be your first time."

Melinda scanned the room again, finding several interesting scenes she wouldn't mind learning more about. "I think this is the perfect distraction to take my mind off what you and your friends found this afternoon."

Seeing all Nick's friends arrive with the sheriff had touched her, and, from the look on Nick's face that she could make out from the window, he, too, was moved by their show of support. The discovery of a possible hiding spot to case out the ranch, and her, left her shaken. She didn't want to bring trouble to Nick, his hands, or his ranch.

Facing her at a barstool, he clasped her waist and lifted her onto the high seat. "Good. I'll do my best to keep your mind off that bastard and on me tonight."

He lifted a hand, and she swiveled to see Amie's husband approaching from behind the bar. She'd met the park ranger at the picnic and noticed he was as protective of his wife as Nick was of Melinda. If only Nick would reveal his emotions as openly as these other men, she could quit second-guessing him.

"Welcome to Spurs, Melinda," Ben greeted her, his green eyes warm and assessing. "What can I get you two?" They both ordered a brew, and, after popping the tabs and squeezing them in koozies, he handed them over.

"Thank you. Is Amie here?" She looked around for her.

"She's out in the hot tub, her favorite spot while I'm bartending or monitoring."

Nick yanked on her hair, the sharp tug on her scalp distracting her from the surprising longing to join Amie, naked if that's what it took to fit in here and make Nick not only proud of her but proud to be with her. "We're not strict on rules around here, darlin', leaving most of them up to each

Dom's preference, but it's best to address them as Sir," he instructed.

Melinda gazed up at Ben, relaxing when he winked. "I'll try to remember. Sir."

"That's all we ask. You can take your drink out to the deck if you wish to join Amie. She's looking forward to seeing you again. Did you hear Lisa went into labor early? Shawn's with her at the hospital."

"I missed that but see it now," Nick replied, looking through his texts.

She lowered her beer and asked Ben, "Is everything going okay? Lisa said she was more than ready two weeks ago but that it was too early."

"As far as I know, there aren't any complications." Someone whistled from the opposite end of the bar, and Ben lifted his hand in acknowledgement. "Catch you two later. Enjoy yourself, Melinda."

"Thank you, Sir." That one rolled off her tongue easily enough, she mused, appreciating Ben's taut backside in snug denim as he strolled down the bar.

"Since you like to ogle, let's see what else catches your eye on the way to the hot tub." Nick tugged her off the stool, and she followed him with a wide grin, the hint of jealousy in his tone thrilling her.

Melinda was grateful for Nick's snug hold of her hand while he explained each apparatus. She found the chain station interesting. The woman bound with her arms stretched above her and her ankles cuffed to a spreader bar swayed with each strike of a leather strap. *Does everyone here get off on pain?* She recalled the arousal heightening effect of Nick's butt slaps, but those seemed tame now compared to the snap of leather. She looked up at Nick as they kept going. "There's a lot to take in, isn't there?"

"For a first time, yes. You're my first newbie, but observing others over the years, I noticed they would either never return or, once they found their niche, they embraced the benefits." He paused at a rocking padded vault, and Melinda's face warmed eyeing the young woman she'd seen with the two men gyrating on the protruding dildo. Squeezing her hand, Nick grinned. "I don't think I've ever seen you turn so red."

"Yeah, well, who wouldn't initially? How

does she do that with her hands tied behind her?" The same two men flanked the vault, watching her struggle to ride the dildo using just her legs to push up and down. Their proud expressions gave Melinda pause, an ache to see Nick looking at her in such a way gripping her.

"I don't know Julie personally," he replied, nodding to the men before nudging Melinda along. "But I'm acquainted with them, and they wouldn't subject her to anything that rigorous if she wasn't physically capable of meeting their expectations. If you decide you want to try something tonight, I suggest a bench, like this one. Hey, Adrian," he greeted the man caressing the blonde's reddened backside as she lay bound facedown on the narrow bench before turning to Melinda. "You met Master Adrian's fiancée, Sophie, at lunch the other day."

Adrian gave her a once-over out of cool gray eyes. "You're Melinda. I heard you had some trouble, Nick. You're welcome to bring your girl to my place for safekeeping."

Melinda stiffened at the way he bypassed her and made the offer to Nick. Before she could retort, Nick intervened.

"We appreciate the offer, but I hope it doesn't come to that. Melinda's not fond of going to safehouses after a bad experience with the last one."

Sophie's buttocks clenched, her need apparent in her swollen, glistening slit even though she remained silent. Maybe it was difficult to talk with her face pressed down on the divided headrest. After hearing about the death of her young daughter and the ordeal someone of Adrian's acquaintance had subjected them both to, Melinda understood how this hard, controlling man's influence had helped her cope. Hadn't she been reaping the same benefits from submitting to Nick's sexual demands? She set her annoyance with Sophie's husband aside enough to reiterate Nick's gratitude.

"Thank you for the offer, Sir. I would love to see your place and your thoroughbreds sometime." Sophie had described the beautiful, expensive, prized horses they bred on their ranch. Melinda would love to see the foals.

"We're planning an engagement party

in the fall. Now, if you'll excuse me." Adrian returned his attention to Sophie.

"Of course." Nick led her toward the glass doors in the back.

Melinda experienced a pang, wondering where she would be come fall then shoved that troubling thought aside for later when she spotted Amie drying off but Skye and Poppy still enjoying the hot tub. If there was one thing that stood out the most since setting foot inside Spurs tonight, it was her escalating desire to please Nick, make him as proud of her as these other men were of their partners.

The calendar said summer, but evenings in Idaho cooled more than she was used to in San Diego. Goose bumps popped up on her arms and legs when they stepped outside, making the swirling, steaming water so enticing, she longed to strip and join her new friends.

"Melinda! Come on in," Poppy invited, her nipples rosy, her breasts floating just above the waterline.

Skye slid down and sent Nick an engaging smile. "We'll watch out for her, Master Nick."

"I don't mind hanging out here for a while if you're needed inside." Melinda hoped he gave her this time to get comfortable baring herself in front of women she was at ease with before she braved doing so in a crowded room of strangers.

"I should see if Clayton or Dakota need help since Shawn is at the hospital. Do you want me to return with your shorts?"

She'd taken off her gym shorts in the foyer, along with her shoes. He was offering an opening to, at least, leave on her panties, which she appreciated. "Sure, thanks."

"Wish I could stay longer, but hubby likes me to keep him company while he's behind the bar." Amie tugged down a thigh-high sheath that clung to her damp body. "Look me up later, Melinda. I'm dying to learn how you like the place." She sailed out with a finger wave, Nick holding the door for her before giving Melinda a thorough kiss then returning inside.

"Whew!" Poppy fanned herself. "Was that lip-lock as hot as it looked?"

Melinda released a dreamy sigh, her lips tingling. "Hotter. Thanks for inviting me to join you." Before she could change her mind or even think about what she was doing, she whipped Nick's shirt over her head and laid it on a bench, her nipples responding to the cooler air with tight puckers. "Oh Lord, this feels good." She groaned, sinking into the hot water, wishing now she had removed her panties also. "Have you heard from Lisa?"

"According to Shawn's last text, she's to the stage of telling him they're never having sex again. He's not taking her seriously, but it's probably good Miss Betty is there," Skye answered.

"And Jerry, which seemed to surprise Miss Betty as much as me," Poppy added.

"Miss Betty? Was she at the picnic?" She didn't recall meeting anyone by that name.

Skye leaned her head back and closed her eyes, saying, "No, Nick just invited our group. Miss Betty is Shawn, Dakota, and Clayton's foster mom. Everyone is fond of Miss Betty."

Poppy grinned. "Including my taciturn, somewhat reclusive boss, Jerry Sanders. They were good friends before each was widowed and just recently have been keeping each other company."

"Sounds nice for everyone." Growing up, Melinda often wished her mother would find a nice man. Now that she had someone to share her golden years with, Melinda couldn't be happier for her.

Skye snorted. "They're doing more than keeping each other company, I'll wager, and," peeking at Poppy, she drawled, "Old Man Sanders is still an ass to everyone except Miss Betty."

"Not me. He's crazy about me."

Poppy frowned, prompting Melinda to ask, "What? You don't care for him liking you so much?"

"Oh no, that's not it." She waved an airy hand, her face turning disgruntled. "It's Dakota. He's driving me nuts, constantly asking if I want to find another job or work with him on the ranch. And lately, he keeps hinting that since my health is finally on the plus side, a baby would be a good challenge for me. What's with that? A baby should be a mutual decision, conceived to start a family with someone you love, not to challenge you. Stupid moron."

Poppy had given Melinda the *Reader's Digest* version of the treatments she'd undergone for cancer followed by a bone marrow transplant that took months to recuperate from. Not knowing Dakota, she kept her opinion to herself and let Skye offer advice.

"C'mon, Poppy. You thrive on challenges to keep from getting bored. According to you, you're surprised you've stuck with Old Man Sanders' manager job this long. It sounds to me like Dakota is fretting over you wanting to take off to try something new, like you used to before coming here."

"I didn't consider that, and, if that's true, he's an even bigger moron," she snapped.

"I can't keep up here." Melinda smiled at Skye.

Poppy held up a finger. "One, he knows me well enough to know I stand by my commitments – meaning him and our marriage. Two." She popped up another finger. "Being married to the strong, silent type isn't easy and a challenge in itself, not to mention the creative ways he comes up with to bang me every chance he gets is enough stimulation for any sane woman. And three." Up went a third digit. "I do believe I would like a baby, not for a challenge, but how cool would that be?" Her blue eyes sparkled, and Skye and Melinda laughed with her until the sudden appearance of a younger woman sobered them.

"Kathie!" Skye straightened and looked behind Kathie, as if seeking why she'd come around the side of the building instead of from inside.

"Hey." Kathie stepped into the light, and they got a good look at her bruised face the same time Neil came out with an angry scowl.

Kathie stepped back as he strode toward her, but he wasn't deterred. Cupping her trembling chin, he held her face up, demanding, "Who did this?"

Her eyes filled with tears, and she darted toward the hot tub. "This was a mistake. I shouldn't have come."

"Of course you should have." Poppy started to rise, but Neil waved her back down.

"I'll handle this. Come with me." Taking Kathie's arm, he left her no choice but to follow him inside.

From the longing etched on her face, Melinda guessed the other girl and this man had a relationship, at least at one time. "Poor girl," she murmured as the door closed behind them.

Skye's face filled with compassion. "Kathie and Master Neil were hooking up regularly before she left for someone she met who wasn't into this lifestyle. Given her love of teasing misbehavior to get a Dom's attention, we all doubted it would last. Master Neil certainly wasn't happy at first."

"And isn't now, either, but he'll take care of her and find out what happened." Poppy turned to Melinda. "Okay, that little drama is over, now, tell us what you think of our club."

"I think all these guys have a protective streak a mile long, which is nice but overwhelming. As for all the different ways to torment someone, I just don't get letting a guy go at you with a strap. I mean, a light hand spanking during sex is titillating, but anything harsher wouldn't be pleasant."

"You don't think so?" Poppy sent Skye an amused look. "Going back to challenges, I think one is in order. What do you think?"

Skye returned her grin then glanced toward the glass doors, drawing Melinda's curiosity. She swiveled on the seat to see Nick, Dakota, and Clayton heading their way.

"First one to climax wins?" Skye asked Poppy.

"That's what I was thinking."

"What are you two talking about?" Melinda didn't trust their mischievous looks, or the way her pulse jumped as the guys joined them outside.

"A spanking contest. The first one of us who orgasms wins," Poppy clarified.

Melinda's incredulous gaze swept from her so-called friends to Nick, who appeared interested in playing their little game. Doubts assailed her, but the light of expectation reflected on the other two men's faces and the pleasant hum their attention on her breasts elicited sealed her decision to grasp this chance to make him proud of her.

"Why not? I'm game to try something different," she agreed before she could change her mind. She almost squealed with delight when Nick's gaze went from astonished to filled with approval.

Chapter Eleven

"I'm always happy to turn Skye over my knees. A game is just what we need to amuse us while we let Neil get to the bottom of what happened to Kathie," Clayton said, winking at his wife.

"If he doesn't get a name from her, I will," Dakota promised in a dark tone, bending to haul Poppy out of the tub as if she weighed nothing. His black gaze slid to Melinda. "Don't let Poppy goad you into anything you aren't comfortable doing."

"Hey! I wouldn't." Poppy smacked his shoulder.

"I trust Nick, so I'm good," she returned, loving Nick's response when he said, "You're just chock-full of surprises tonight, aren't you, darlin'?"

Before she could answer, he sat on a

bench and flipped her over his lap. The breath *whooshed* out of her then caught on a gasp with the bounce of his palm off her wet, panty-covered cheek. Warmth infused her, both from the arousal-stimulating prickles and the bare-flesh-smacking echo resonating in the open air. She'd never imagined herself an exhibitionist, but she'd never found herself in such an erotic state of escalating excitement. Nick delivered several light spanks, each generating a touch more heat than the previous and a deeper, pleasant ache that never failed to feed into her lust. She'd enjoyed the same buildup every other time he'd paid such attention to her backside, only, this time, the public inclusion of others provided an additional adrenaline rush she found herself embracing.

Melinda squirmed on his lap, Poppy and Skye's whimpers changing to grunts while she remained behind, still wearing panties. Without thinking about it, she reached behind her and yanked her panties down, removing the thin barrier and exposing herself fully to the others. Nick laid a hand on one bare buttock, and she groaned from the sheer pleasure of skin-on-skin contact and knowing others were watching. Exhibitionism seemed to work for her.

Nick squeezed her cheek, bending over to whisper near her ear. "Do you trust me enough to win this?"

"Yes," she replied without hesitation, already aching for release as much as the desire to not only fit in but make him proud. "Go for it."

"That's my girl."

His low-murmured approval followed by a steady application of soft butt taps covering both buttocks sent her senses soaring. She latched onto his leg to anchor herself against the building pleasure, her entire body quivering with expectancy. The same warmth she'd experienced before spread across her butt, increasing her arousal but not enough to wring an orgasm from her. Just when she despaired of making a fool of herself, he delivered a much harder smack, the burn and pain seeping into muscle.

"Oh!" Melinda exclaimed under her breath, the next one coming fast and with hard enough impact to threaten her balance.

Nick scooped an arm around her waist, the much-needed support giving her the freedom to concentrate solely on this new experience.

Each slap landed harder than the last, the soft pulses of discomfort slowly morphing into a deeper, throbbing pain. She bit her lip, not sure if she wanted to call a stop or beg for more when her backside turned puffy, went numb from the harsher spanks that pushed her pelvis against his muscled thigh. Then ripples of pleasure started tickling her pussy with each abrasive contact against the soft, unprotected flesh of her bare labia, every rub against his rock-hard thigh increasing the tremors building deep inside her core, making the decision for her.

Nick paused to caress her sore cheeks and run a finger along her pussy lips before resuming his spanking with lighter smacks that emphasized the tender pangs. She had tuned out the others, too engrossed with the flood of new sensations derived from the throbbing pain to think about anything else. Familiar need drummed throughout her lower body, her arousal heightening to an unexpected, exalted high yet still teetering just short of orgasm.

Melinda shook as he slid downward to belabor the sensitive area under the curved, plumpness of each buttock, the burn spreading down to her thighs. Her breathing grew heavy with each grind of her pelvis on his leg, increasing the pressure in her groin. She went giddy as those wonderful small contractions erupted, hinting at release until Nick shocked her into an intense, full-blown orgasm with a sharp slap on the tender flesh of her labia. The searing agony sent waves of pleasure through her arching body, a sob tearing from her throat from the sudden, mind-and-body-encompassing release.

"A three-way tie?"

Untold moments later, Clayton's amused tone snuck through the euphoric fog still filling Melinda's head as Nick turned her over and cuddled her on his lap. "That was my take," he said, his deep voice rumbling under her ear placed against his chest.

I can really get used to this. Melinda sighed, not caring about the challenge, only about holding on to the pleasant afterglow from that wild ride. Her butt and labia both throbbed, the slight aches not the least bothersome or off-putting. *Go figure.* She certainly couldn't make heads or tails out of reaping such a reward from that harsher discomfort.

"If we're done here, I have a few words to say to my wife." Dakota didn't sound happy, and when Melinda peeked one eye open, she saw he didn't look happy as he flipped Poppy over his shoulder. "I also intend to grill Neil about our Kathie."

"Copy that," Clayton replied, running a hand up and down Skye's thigh.

Their words were laced with grim retribution, along with Nick's as he said, "I'll meet you back downstairs in an hour to join in on that talk. While Neil is seeing to Kathie's needs, though, I'm going upstairs to finish what I started here."

Melinda was all for that and didn't notice him reaching for the T-shirt until he slipped it over her head and stood with her in his arms. Cool air wafted over her exposed butt, raising goose bumps across her still-burning cheeks. Sighing, she looped her arms around his neck, content enough to let him carry her through the main room and up the stairs with her reddened buttocks left uncovered. The enjoyable aftershocks from her off-the-charts climax were still rolling through her, offering something to concentrate on besides her vulnerable state. She was so ecstatic over her successful participation in a scene, she didn't mind the knowing smiles from onlookers.

When Nick reached the second floor and entered a room, she roused enough to stop him from kicking the door shut. "No. Leave it open. I won't mind if anyone walks by." Glancing up, she couldn't miss the stark hunger etched on his face, the lustful need swirling in his chocolate eyes. A desire to give back for a change instead of letting him take her over again took hold as he dropped her onto the four-poster bed. She flung off the shirt and waited until he stripped and joined her before springing up with a wicked grin. "My turn," she insisted, straddling his hips and pressing her hands on his chest. "Stay put."

Lifting a brow, he scanned her face then nodded, his lips curling in a taunting grin.

"You have my permission, darlin'."

She snorted and reached between her legs to wrap a hand around his cock. "I didn't ask for permission, but hey, go ahead and tell me no, don't do this." Sliding down, she took him in her mouth, chuckling around his hard flesh when he sucked in a deep breath with a low curse.

Craving to give back a portion of what he'd given her, Melinda drew on his rigid erection like a woman possessed, and maybe she was because she couldn't get enough of him. She raked her teeth along the swollen, throbbing veins, and Nick gripped her hair. Her tongue snaked around his smooth crown to swipe over his seeping slit before dipping underneath to tease those hidden sensitive tissues, and he clamped his other hand on her shoulder. His dual hold worked as well as any aphrodisiac and she mumbled, "*Yes*," around his engorged flesh. She took him deep then pulled up against his grip, the struggle a kinky turn-on she embraced. It soon became a battle of wills between her sucking hard enough for him to loosen his grip and him trying to hold her still for his thrusts.

Nick either tired of the game before her or thought he would lose when he quickened in her mouth because he hauled her up without warning and ground his mouth on hers. Melinda returned his aggressive kiss with just as much voracious hunger, loving his crushing weight as he rolled her onto her back. She never tired of running her hands over his smooth, bulging muscles, of his strength pinning her to the bed before he would restrain one or two limbs.

"This bed has a slew of binding options," he rasped above her lips. "I can get creative with three restraints."

Since the first time he had introduced her to bondage, he'd always left at least one of her hands free. She guessed it was to give her a sense of control even though they were both aware he could overpower her regardless. Maybe it was the last two weeks of him not pushing for full sexual control that enabled her to enjoy so much of her first night at the club. Whatever the reason, she wanted to prove he'd more than earned her complete trust again.

"Let's go for four."

Nick didn't think Melinda could surprise him again tonight, but he was wrong. Her final concession to admitting a full return of faith in him again couldn't have been pronounced more eloquently. His swollen cock jerked as he contemplated his options, pre-cum still dripping from the hard suction of her mouth and soft press of her lips.

"Scoot up," he instructed, having settled on how he wanted to take her.

Melinda scrambled upward, her bright-blue eyes widening, her face reddening as he cuffed her wrists and raised her arms up and out toward the top of the bedposts.

He kissed her, tasting himself on her tongue before shifting back. "Hang tight for a minute."

"I don't think I have much choice," she returned wryly, tugging on her arms.

"You always have a choice," he reminded her, pulling out a strap from under the mattress and wrapping it around her thigh. "Don't forget."

After binding her other thigh, Nick suited up and pressed a button on the side of the bed, elevating her against the wall with her knees bent, feet left dangling. Eyeing her gaping pussy and the damp, pink swath beckoning his cock, he knelt between her spread thighs and clasped her still-warm cheeks. "Nice," he breathed against her mouth, gliding his cock between her folds.

"Nick, Sir, please, don't..." Small white teeth clamped down on her lower lip as he slid inside her real slow, savoring her tight, wet welcoming grip.

"Don't what?" Digging his fingers into her ass, he rocked her on his cock, sliding her forward then back, loving the tight squeezes around his erection sure to set him off.

"I was going to say don't make me...wait, but...you're...*oh God*." She groaned, her head thumping against the wall, her eyes closing as he increased his steady plunges deep inside her.

"Couldn't, even if I wanted to." Nick took her harder, faster, yanking her pelvis back and forth, his chest heaving along with hers, their heavy breathing and the suction of their bodies coming together the only sounds in the room. He could barely hear the music and voices from downstairs now, his concentration focused on wringing another climax from her before his giving in to his own release.

The quickening of her slick, damp muscles rippling around his cock came seconds before he jerked with the first streams jetting from his cockhead. Her soft cries joined with his heavy grunts, his orgasm raging like a wildfire through his system. Nick waited for his head to start clearing before slowing his pace, taking time to relish the puffy contractions still fluttering along his cock.

Coming to terms with his soul-deep feelings for Melinda and deciding where to go from here would take a little longer.

Pulling out of her snug warmth, he took in her flushed, sated face and closed eyes with wry amusement and a slow roll of his heart. "Are you conscious?"

"Barely." She sighed the word, and he leaned forward to kiss her satisfied grin. She opened her eyes and scanned his close face. A touch of worry turned the vivid blue darker, but the determined set of her jaw was familiar and as welcome as her next words. "We have to talk."

"I agree." Nick released her legs then her arms, and she lowered them with a wince. "Are you okay?"

Melinda patted his chest. "I'm fine, just unaccustomed to all the physical activity. Not just the marathon sex but the daily riding." She brushed a finger over his nipple, the light graze sending a zap of electric pleasure down to his balls. "I feel well used and love every ache."

Nick rolled off the bed before he made the mistake of taking that well-used body again. "Give me a minute and I'll help you wash up and dress." He nodded toward the attached bathroom.

"Nonsense." Before he could stop her, she slid off on the other side and sprinted into the bathroom, her hair swaying around the middle of her back, her pink buttocks standing out against the stark black braid and her otherwise pale skin. Hand on the door, she swiveled her head, giving him a mischievous look. "FYI, *Master* Nick, the sex is freaking awesome, but I'm still perfectly capable of washing myself and dressing."

Melinda shut the door and he heard the lock engage. Nick disposed of the condom and used bottled water from the mini fridge and tissues to take care of himself, admitting he loved her feisty, independent side as much as her willingness to submit to his sexual demands.

She was perfect for him. He'd known that in Cheyenne when someone had robbed them of the chance to explore their connection and enhance the bond they'd developed during those two months. Given this second chance, he wouldn't allow that person's actions to drive another wedge between them, which he intended to make clear when they had their talk.

Since he had her shirt and gym shorts, he gave her no choice but to let him help her when she emerged from the bathroom. "Okay," she said as he escorted her downstairs, "that battle of wills was a draw."

"I can live with that." Nick spotted Dakota and Clayton at the bar, and Neil headed toward them with a grim look. He nodded toward the three girls seated at a table. "Do you mind joining Skye, Poppy, and Kathie while I get in on the powwow about Kathie's injuries?"

"Not at all." Melinda glanced at Kathie's bruised face, concern clouding her gaze. "I don't know her, but no woman deserves that."

Nick agreed. "No worries. We take care of our own, as you saw earlier today on your behalf."

Kathie's eyes were glued on Neil, and she didn't seem to notice them approaching when she said, "I've never seen him so angry."

Poppy patted Kathie's hand lying on the table. "He's tried to hide it, but he wasn't happy when you hooked up with Mr. Vanilla Asshole."

"Not in the least," Nick stated, holding the empty chair for Melinda. In the year he'd been a member, he'd never seen the perky mischief-maker so subdued. The anger churning inside him at seeing her bruised face reminded him of his volatile reaction when he'd found Melinda in that warehouse. He set a bottled water in front of her. "Finish that. I'll return shortly."

Pivoting, he strode to the bar before she could get into trouble by laying into him for that order. He'd always been good at reading her expressions.

"What did I miss?" Nick straddled a stool and faced Neil whose thunderous expression spoke volumes.

"Our girl picked the wrong guy to try a committed, vanilla relationship with," Clayton answered.

"And do we have a plan?" Nick had come to know these men well enough to appreciate their united front whenever they witnessed abuse of any kind toward anyone.

"I doubt Shawn will look the other way if I beat the son of a bitch to a pulp, but it would be worth risking the legal repercussions." Neil kicked back the rest of his straight whiskey as Ben handed Nick a beer from behind the bar.

"We figure we'll all pay him a visit and set him straight." Ben's green gaze cut to Neil. "And to keep him in line."

A rare smile softened Dakota's tough face. "And another one bites the dust."

Neil's brows snapped together in a

frown. "What's that supposed to mean?"

Clayton rolled his eyes. "C'mon, Neil. You've only had half your head in the game since she left, and the way you can't keep your eyes off her now speaks for you."

Neil rolled his eyes, as if Clayton was full of shit. "I've never denied I'm fond of her, but she's too young, and her constant mischief-making can be annoying."

"Yeah, you keep telling yourself that, partner," Ben drawled.

Nick experienced a pang hearing Ben tease his park ranger partner. He and Mike used to banter back and forth like that, his partner ribbing him over his growing attachment to Melinda and him denying it until it was too late. He glanced toward her, his chest aching at the thought of losing her again.

"Speaking of another one biting the dust," Clayton murmured, nudging Nick. "You stay close to your girl tomorrow while we take care of Kathie's abuser."

Neil blew out a breath and shook his head, looking from Kathie's bruised face toward Nick. "Okay, there's no use in either of us arguing with these guys. I plan to make sure this jerk doesn't come near Kathie again and then I'm willing to stay open to seeing how far our relationship can go. How about you?"

Nick didn't have to mull over his answer. "I already lost her once. I won't risk doing so again." He downed the rest of his beer and set the bottle on the bar top. "Let me know how it goes tomorrow."

Returning to the table, he clasped Melinda's arm and nudged her to her feet. "If you'll excuse us, ladies, we need to get going."

Clayton's voice came over the loudspeaker just then, grabbing everyone's attention with his announcement. "It's a boy!"

The room resounded with cheers, clapping, and whistles, and Nick took the opportunity to slip out without further delays. As soon as he pulled out onto the main road, Melinda turned to him with an inquisitive tilt of her head. "Are we in a hurry for any particular reason?"

"Yes, a long, overdue talk."

She settled back in the seat, surprising him when she stated, "Then let me start by saying I'm going to testify."

Surprised, he slammed on the brakes, easing to the side of the road before whipping sideways to face her in the darkened cab. "Are you sure?"

"Yes, but only under one condition. I stay here, with you, where I'm safer than in a safehouse in Cheyenne, until the new trial."

After all this time believing she would be better off testifying than running or living in limbo, hearing her say she would do so now sent a chill skating down his spine. He experienced the same reaction whenever his sixth sense kicked in, warning him of possible danger, but this time without those prickles of awareness. He figured that meant she wasn't in immediate danger. At least, that's what he hoped.

Getting back on the road, Nick forced himself to agree, vowing he would keep her safe this time around. "I'll send Honeycutt and the DA a message in the morning. They'll get it even though it's the weekend. As it happens, you beat me to it – I was going to start our talk by asking you to stay." He reached over and squeezed her trembling fingers. "Nervous?"

"I'm not stupid, so yes." She turned her hand in his and held tight. "But I am confident you'll protect me."

"Damn straight."

****

Cortez wanted to ignore his phone when he saw the caller was his lawyer. Pissed-off frustration didn't begin to describe his mood since he'd driven out to his cozy hiding spot yesterday only to discover a group of men looking around. Their grim faces spoke louder than words, and he'd kept going, giving up on his revenge to play it safe. First, it had been that schmuck, Phillips, surviving his overdose, and now, this failure.

Tossing his shirts into the open suitcase on the motel bed, he swore when his phone kept buzzing. Snatching it off the nightstand, he didn't bother hiding his irritation.

"What now, Carmichael?"

"You better be nicer to me, Cortez, if you

want to stay out of prison."

Cortez paced the dingy carpet wishing Alan Carmichael stood in front of him. Spilling blood would suit him just fine right about now. "Again, you prick, what do you want? I'm not telling you where I am." His lawyer was privy to most of his secrets but not all of them.

"You're not the only one with snitches on your payroll. Mine in the DA's office passed me a juicy tidbit you're not going to like."

"On a Sunday? How reliable can this person be, or the information?"

"Damned reliable since she's sleeping with him and was there when he got a call from Captain Honeycutt telling him to prepare for trial. Walsh has decided to testify again."

Every muscle in Cortez's body contracted with the icy-cold rage consuming him. In a fit of temper, he swung out his arm and sent the bedside lamp crashing against the wall. *Un-fucking believable!* Could anything else go wrong?

"What are you going to do about this?" he growled into the phone, expecting his lawyer to pull a miracle out of his hat.

"All I can do is try to discredit her on the stand. It's not my fault you offed someone in front of a witness. Come to my office this week, and we'll come up with a game plan."

Not likely.

He hung up without answering, intending to end this today. Canada might not extradite him for drug charges, but they would for murder. No witness, no proof, no charges. He finished packing and checked out, paying cash for the whole bill. The manager never asked for his ID, but he had one as fake as the name he'd given when he checked in just in case.

Cortez drove toward the ranch where Walsh had found refuge, determined to do whatever was necessary to rid himself of her threat.

Chapter Twelve

Melinda leaned against the one kitchen counter Nick had installed and sipped her coffee, watching him pace the hardwood floor with his phone to his ear. He wore nothing but jeans with the snap at the waist left open and she couldn't look at his wide shoulders and that bronzed, sculpted chest with the light smattering of black curls without thinking about last night. Would she ever get used to the erotic thrill of such focused attention on her needs or the exultant pleasure she continued to reap from his possession, and just his? She was sore this morning, her muscles aching, her buttocks tender, her pussy sensitive to even the warm washcloth, yet she stood here practically drooling for more.

Sometime between embracing

everything he'd subjected her to and his comforting aftercare, she'd decided she was done with Cortez running her life. He'd scared her off two years ago, and she'd lost something she hadn't realized she wanted so much.

Nick.

Her fingers itched to smooth the worry lines around his eyes as he kept glancing at her while he talked to Captain Honeycutt. He'd awoken edgy, constantly checking in with Spenser and Jose, his voice terse as he grilled his former boss on the investigation into their leak. He wasn't this unsettled last night, and she wondered if there was something he was keeping from her. If so, there was no time like the present to set him straight on a few things if she stayed.

"So, there's some good news, then. Okay. You'll let me know? Thanks, Captain."

Nick clicked off and set the phone on the table then tunneled his fingers through his hair, offering a glimpse of his underarm hair. God, she went hot, even finding his armpits sexy. She was either sick or in love.

She went with in love. All the more

reason to let him know she wouldn't accept being kept in the dark about anything that concerned her.

"What's wrong, Melinda?" Nick stepped in front of her, forcing her head up to gaze at his concerned face. "Are you having second thoughts about testifying, or staying here?"

"Neither." She placed a hand on his chest, wishing Cortez behind bars so they could get on with their lives. "Tell me what Captain Honeycutt said, and what's bothering you this morning."

"You mean other than my job to keep you safe? Isn't that enough?"

"You've held that position for two weeks now and weren't this tense," she reminded him.

Nick hesitated, looking unsure, which worried her because he was rarely unsure about himself. "Honeycutt is glad you changed your mind and will meet with the DA in the morning. He didn't like the idea of you staying here, but, as you heard, I told him tough, that wasn't negotiable."

She remembered his implacable tone when he'd said that. "Even I think twice before arguing with you when you use that voice."

Bracing his hands on the counter at her hips, he caged her in and leaned forward to tug on her lower lip with his teeth, the sharp prick zinging straight down to her toes. "And yet, most times you go ahead and give me your two cents."

"Someone has to stand up to you." Her breathing hitched as he tongued the small throb but she stiffened and pressed against his chest. He didn't budge, frustrating her. "Nick, talk to me."

He blew out a breath, giving her a peevish look before nodding and stepping back. "Fine, but if you laugh or think I'm nuts, I'll dig out the wooden spoon."

Melinda winced, yet her buttocks clenched and her pussy dampened. She would have to rethink if she was sick. "I won't. What's going on?"

She listened as he explained the odd sensations he would get before something bad or tragic happened, going back to when they first started and the incidents that occurred. When he waited for her reaction, she said the first thing that popped in her head. "That is so cool. And you're getting those prickles this morning?"

Appreciation softened his face, but it was the deep emotion in his dark eyes that caused her stomach to flip-flop. "You continue to amaze me, darlin'." He leaned in again and cupped her face. "No wonder I love you so much." He covered her gaping mouth with his, and she melted into his kiss, his simple declaration all she needed to hear to seal her fate.

Nick released her and stepped back again, not giving her a chance to say anything as he said, "To answer your question, yes, since I woke up, which is why we're staying here for now. Ben, Neil, and Dakota are taking turns over the next few days scouting the woods surrounding my property, at least until we hear back from the DA on a trial date." He pivoted to fill a mug with coffee, saying over his shoulder, "I have to get to work. Do you want to stay inside or hang around the stables?"

"I'll go out. I want to see how Merry is doing after the fire scare. And, Nick?" She waited until he faced her again before telling him softly, "You had me at hello."

He flashed her one of his devastating grins as he started toward the bedroom, she assumed to finish dressing. "I'm a hell of a lot luckier than *Jerry Maguire*."

"And don't you forget it," she said to his back. Despite the upheaval of her life, Melinda hadn't felt this positive about the future in over a year.

Melinda stood at the fence, watching Nick work one of his quarter horses scheduled for pickup this week, all too aware of the pistol tucked into his pants and the rifles Spenser and Jose were carrying. She glanced down at her firearm leaning against the rail, wondering if she could pull the trigger on another person. She prayed she didn't have to find out.

Shielding her eyes, she glanced toward Merry then stood stock-still, holding her breath, shocked to see the mare walking slowly right up to the fence. This was the first time Merry had come to her without her holding out a carrot bribe to lure her over. As much as she wanted to, she didn't try to pet her, instead, reaching into her pocket for the carrot she never came out here without. The mare took it gently, not leaving as she chewed, those beautiful, wary eyes remaining steadfast on Melinda's face.

"Hey, sweetheart, how's my girl?"

Merry nudged her arm, the first time she'd ever attempted contact. Swallowing her trepidation, Melinda lifted a shaking hand to stroke the mare's scarred neck, releasing her held breath when Merry seemed comfortable with her touch.

"Well, I'll be damned."

Melinda looked behind her, smiling at Spenser and Jose who stood there agape as she continued to stroke Merry's damaged neck. "I know, I couldn't believe it either. She came right up to me when she saw me here. I didn't even have the carrot out to bribe her. Has she been okay since the fire?"

"None of the horses have shown signs of fear or trauma."

Spenser kept his voice pitched low and Merry remained at the fence, but the skittish mare backed away with a whinny and shake of her head as the two guys approached.

"Sorry," Jose muttered, watching Merry's retreat with regret.

"No, don't be. I'm thrilled with every small step forward she takes. I wish I could ride her, but she's coming along, isn't she?" She sighed, hearing the wistful regret in her voice.

"You bet." Spenser leaned against the fence and nudged his hat back. "Better than what we were getting. You must have a magic touch, or voice."

"No." Melinda resisted the urge to touch her scarred face. "Just someone who can feel her pain. It looks like you're almost done shoring up the stable." The two had been here first thing this morning to reinforce the stable's charred boards until the contractors could replace the entire side. "Nick's going to owe you overtime."

"He's a good man, our boss," Jose said.

"Yes, he is," she murmured, watching Nick riding the horse out of the pasture, his phone once again held to his ear.

Since she'd decided to testify, the weight pressing down on Melinda's shoulders from the moment she'd learned Cortez was out of prison was much lighter. Whether it was wishful thinking or her restored faith in Nick, it didn't matter at this point. She would take what she could get when she could. She took in Nick's perspiring face and neck as he strode toward her, not needing to see his eyes under the Stetson to know he was focused on her. She would take her cowboy any day of the week, and any way she could get him.

"Did I just see you touching Merry?" Nick asked, his tone as surprised as Melinda had felt.

"You sure did, boss," Jose beamed, as if it was his accomplishment.

"Well, will wonders never cease. That seals the deal, then, darlin'. Now you'll have to stick around." Nick gave her a smug look.

"I guess I will." She sent him a cheeky grin, wishing they could go riding and play in the woods again. "Who was on the phone that made you scowl?"

Nick cut his gaze toward his hands. "Ben found an injured calf separated from the herd. He's down with a bad sprain and needs to be picked up. You two take the truck out there, and Ben will wait to help load him.

Keep your rifles handy."

Spenser looked concerned as he replied, "Are you sure you'll be okay until we get back?"

"We'll be fine, but thanks," Nick said. "I need to finish the paperwork for Samson's new owners, so we'll be at the house by the time you return."

"It won't take us long," Jose added before following Spenser to the truck.

"You have great employees. You don't suspect foul play?" Melinda wouldn't put anything past Cortez, up to and including harming an innocent animal to draw them out in the open. She'd suffered a harsh lesson in not underestimating the extent of Cortez's evil.

"No, but it never hurts to stay alert. Ben said the calf went down near a gopher or prairie dog's hole that he probably got tripped up on. Come on. You can help me groom Samson so he looks his best for the Andersons."

****

Things were finally going Cortez's way today. He had been about to whip a U-turn on the back road adjacent to the Rossi ranch when he spotted a ranger's cruiser coming his way. Before he could execute the turn, the cruiser veered into the open range, bouncing toward a black lump that turned out to be a calf. Taking advantage of the man's distraction, Cortez kept going, getting as close to the barns as possible without being seen. As soon as he glimpsed the roofs through the trees, he pulled over, intending to make this quick. From his previous surveillance, he knew Rossi only employed two hands. As he crept through the trees, a surge of sadistic satisfaction whipped through him watching the two cowhands drive off, presumably to fetch the disabled calf.

"Who said crime doesn't pay?" he muttered with glee, his gaze scoping the stable yard for the two people who were the cause of all his troubles. He lifted his rifle and took aim the same moment Rossi jerked his head toward him and shouted for Walsh to get down.

Cortez pulled the trigger, not taking the

time to question what had alerted the cop to his presence. Walsh dove inside the stable as his bullet struck Rossi, her cry reaching Cortez the same time a bullet whizzed by his head and slammed into the tree next to him. The second she dropped her rifle to bend over Rossi, he ran forward, spraying bullets around her firearm as soon as she saw him and went for it again.

"Gotcha, bitch," he snarled, kicking the gun out of her reach then sticking his in her face. He wasn't prepared for her to come after him like a woman possessed.

Melinda's scream helped Nick rouse through the searing pain covering his entire shoulder. Grabbing his gun, he forced himself to his knees, his gaze swinging toward the field where he saw her fighting Cortez's hold tooth and nail, her struggles preventing him from getting off a shot.

"That's my girl," he murmured, struggling to his feet to take aim. He stumbled forward, intending to get as close as possible, let her know to give him a chance to shoot, but an angry whinny caught all three of their attention first.

Nick was stunned to see Merry charging Cortez, the mare clamping her big teeth on the arm holding Melinda. Cortez's scream reverberated in the air, and Nick could see the spurt of blood as he rushed forward, guessing she'd snapped the bone from the way he dropped Melinda's arm with an agonized cry.

Melinda didn't even notice him approaching, bending to grab Cortez's gun from where he'd dropped it, her hand shaking as she tried calling Merry off her attacker. "Merry, c...come he...here, girl."

Nick reached them as Merry backed off and Cortez fell to the ground, sobbing in agony, cradling his shattered arm. "Melinda. Come on, darlin', put the gun down."

She took her eyes off her nemesis long enough to give him a concerned once-over then shook her head, aiming for Cortez's head. "He killed m...my father, and put m... me through he...hell."

Nick gazed at her ashen, scarred face, his heart aching for all she'd been through. If he thought killing Cortez would give her closure, he'd let her pull the trigger. But it would only add to the burden she'd been carrying these many months.

"Yes, he did, but imagine the satisfaction you'll get saying that in court, and then hearing him get life without parole, of knowing from here on out, he'll be the one suffering, not you, not us."

"Pull the fucking trigger," Cortez rasped, not even trying to stand.

Melinda dropped her arm, turning her tear-streaked face to Nick, took in his injury, and tucked the gun in her waist. He'd never been so proud of her as when she straightened her shoulders and stated in a steady voice, "Don't take your eye off him," then pulled her shirt over her head to form a wrap for his shoulder.

"Melinda." He winced, lifting his injured arm enough for her to knot the shirt, never taking his eyes off Cortez, who now lay cowed by his own pain. "This can wait. I'm fine. We need to..." The roar of vehicles rumbling toward them drew all their attention, and Nick recognized Ben's grim face in his cruiser, Spenser and Jose right behind him.

"I was going to say we need to get help."

Melinda was too grateful for the guys' arrival to be embarrassed standing there in her bra when Ben and the guys leaped from their vehicles as soon as they stopped. Her concern was more for Nick and Merry than her modesty. Everything had happened so fast, the sequence of events were kind of blurry. One minute, she and Nick were walking into the stable, the next, he went rigid, swore, and ordered her down as he drew his gun. The sight and smell of blood covering his shoulder had sent her into full panic, her first thought she couldn't lose him, not again. When Cortez had grabbed her, his intent to shut her up permanently as clear as her feelings for Nick, she'd simply let go of months of suppressed anger and despair.

As the men gathered around, all talking at once, she searched for Merry and found her standing still several yards away, her stance of wary distrust breaking Melinda's heart. The poor horse likely thought they would turn on her for her attack on a person. Melinda took a step toward her only to stop when a shirt was laid over her shoulders. She looked up at Ben as she slipped her arms into the sleeves, giving him a slow smile of appreciation, enjoying the view of his bare chest. "Thanks."

"You're welcome. Let's get you guys up to the house. More help is on the way," he said just as the faint wail of sirens reached their ears.

"Give her a minute," Nick instructed, nodding at Melinda to go to Merry. "Meet us at the house. It'll be a few minutes of chaos when the cavalry arrives, so you have time to thank and reassure her."

Once again, he was seeing to her needs before his own, and she wondered why she'd ever mistrusted him. At least with Cortez out of the way, she would have ample time to give back to him as much as he'd given her.

Melinda approached Merry with caution, talking to her, expressing her gratitude and telling her how proud she was of her. Merry stood stock-still, not running off, keeping those soft eyes fixated on Melinda. When she halted in front of her, she reached out a tentative hand and stroked her nose. Tears clogged her throat when Merry leaned into her with a snort, not only accepting her touch but begging for more attention.

"If you follow me in, I'll get you your treat. And just so you know"—Melinda sifted through her mane hanging over her marred neck—"I'm telling Nick to forget sending you to a sanctuary. Neither one of us needs another upheaval in our lives, do we, baby?"

She cupped Merry's snout and tugged, hoping she took the hint to come with her as she started toward the stable. Melinda went giddy with pleasure when Merry fell in step with her, and she treated her with several carrots as the cops and ambulance arrived. Hurrying up to the house, she breathed a sigh of relief seeing Nick getting treated by one of the paramedics while the other one went to the porch where Cortez was handcuffed to the post.

"You can give me a statement later," Shawn was saying, his gray eyes concerned when the paramedic bared Nick's wounded shoulder.

Melinda grew light-headed seeing the amount of blood loss, but Nick's sharp voice propelled her forward. "Melinda, come here."

He held out his good arm, and she gripped his hand. "How bad is it?"

"The bullet went through, which is easier than surgery but makes for even more blood loss." Nick glared at the attendant, and he sent Melinda a reassuring smile. "He'll be fine, ma'am. I'll suture both wounds closed before we transport him to the hospital for further evaluation."

"Don't argue," Shawn ordered when Nick appeared ready to do just that.

Nick scowled. "Shouldn't you be home nagging your wife and tending to your new son?"

"Yes, but I got tagged to join in on confronting Kathie's abuser this morning, and, right after that fun, I got an SOS from Ben. Lisa understands, so deal with it." Shawn crossed his arms in a belligerent pose.

"Listen to them, Nick. Please. We have a lot to do, and you need to be up to par." She lifted a brow and cocked her head, knowing just how to get to him. "Unless you want me to return to Cheyenne without you."

"You even try and I'll..." He clamped his

mouth shut when Shawn cleared his throat with a meaningful glance at the paramedic. "I'll go in, but I'm not riding in with that asshole." He jerked his head toward Cortez. "He can have the ambulance. Melinda and I will hitch a ride in with you, and you can tell us what went down with that prick this morning," he told Shawn.

"That I'll agree to."

****

Two weeks later

"Are you sure?" Nick stared at the closed door to Owen Phillips' hospital room, still unable to believe the detective he'd worked with and trusted for the last decade had betrayed them. "Why did he do it?" he asked his former captain.

Captain Honeycutt appeared as devastated by the news as Nick. "He confessed, and, as to why, he went off the deep end after his divorce two years ago, gambling, drinking, even drugs. It didn't take long for things to spiral out of control and, by then, Cortez had him over a barrel, or so he claims."

"There's no fucking excuse good enough. Mike's dead because of him." Nick glanced down at Melinda's hand on his good arm then at the compassion etched on her face, the sadness in her eyes. "Why aren't you as pissed as I am?" His shoulder still ached, and he was stuck wearing a sling for another week, constant reminders of the additional consequences Phillips' betrayal had put them through.

"Because getting angry won't change anything, and I'm too relieved at finally being able to put all this behind me without fear to waste the energy. Go." Melinda nodded toward the door. "Do what you have to do. I'll wait out here."

"You don't want to confront the man who caused you such grief?" He couldn't believe she didn't have a few choice words for Phillips. Nick certainly did.

She shook her head and dropped her hand. "From what the captain has said, Detective Phillips' remorse is genuine, and his grief is just starting. Even I am aware of the difficult time ahead of him as a cop going to prison."

That was true, and since Owen was responsible for another cop's death, he was looking at life, the same as Cortez had agreed to in order to avoid the death penalty. "We won't be long."

Owen opened his eyes as Nick and Honeycutt entered his hospital room then closed them again when he saw him. *Tough,* Nick thought, closing the door, hardening his heart against the ravaged appearance of his once friend. He wasn't about to let him off easy.

"Are you and the girl all right?" Owen asked, his voice weak and resigned.

"No thanks to you. I'm glad we didn't take Cortez out, otherwise, you wouldn't have confessed, would you?" He couldn't think of another reason for Owen to come clean after all this time.

Lifting his eyelids, Owen's gaze went to their captain. He ignored Nick's question, saying, "I never told Cortez, but I left a sealed confession with my attorney, instructing him to open it upon my death. Thank you for talking to the DA. They have agreed to incarcerate me in a separate facility from Cortez." He sighed and twisted his hands in the sheets before looking back at Nick. "For what it's worth, I am sorry and would appreciate it if you would let Ms. Walsh know I regret what happened. Cortez promised me no one would get hurt; he just wanted her out of the way until I could help him flee the country. It was stupid to trust him."

"Ms. Walsh might forgive you, but I'm thinking Mike Reynolds' widow and kids won't be so willing," Honeycutt answered.

Nick couldn't stomach standing there another minute, not with Melinda waiting for him and a future ahead of them they could finally embrace now that they both had closure. "Good luck, Owen," was all he said, thinking he would need it wherever he was going.

Captain Honeycutt followed him out of the room, and Nick held out his hand. "Sorry I once suspected you."

He shook his hand. "You were at the top of my list. You do know both Cortez and

Phillips planned for you to take the fall by taking out Reynolds and wounding Owen."

"Yeah, I figured as much." Another reason Nick refused to accept Owen's regrets. He glanced at Melinda as she joined them, the compassion and love in her vivid blue eyes all he needed to get over his colleague's betrayal. If she could move past the consequences of that night, then so could he. Unable to resist, he ignored Honeycutt and the hospital staff looking their way. Cupping her face, he rested his forehead against hers. "The stuff that dreams are made of."

Melinda's slow smile brushed his lips. Eager to get out of there, Nick grabbed her hand and walked toward the elevator as she asked, "Are you quoting Sam Spade from the *Maltese Falcon*, or Shakespeare from *The Tempest*?"

He punched the button, giving her a rueful look. "Only you would know that line was first used in *The Tempest*. But does it matter?"

"Nope, not in the least. I love you, too."

"Let's go home, darlin'."

Doms of Mountain Bend Epilogue

Three months later

The nip in the air hinted at fall but the sun shone bright and high in the blue Idaho sky for the final picnic of the season. Neighbors from Mountain Bend and the surrounding ranches converged on the Rolling Hills Ranch, their vehicles lining the long drive leading up to the old farmhouse once owned by Buck and Betty Cooper. Father Joe sat in the front porch rocker, gazing down at Shawn's infant son, his heart swelling with emotion.

Patrick Joseph McDuff.

Our boy has done both of us proud, my friend.

He'd had the pleasure of baptizing his best friend's grandson this morning and was further blessed when Dakota and Clayton both announced their impending fatherhoods. By this time next year, two more babies would join little Patrick and the other baby whose mother waylaid him as soon as he arrived back here from the church. Joe scanned the tables where guests were enjoying the homemade cooking of their neighbors and spotted the strawberry blonde, Mickie, laughing as she hopped with Poppy in the three-legged race. He replayed their introduction with fondness.

"You're Father Joe, right?" the petite, gray-eyed young woman asked when Joe entered the kitchen.

"I am. And you are?"

"Mickie Daniels. Huh, still can't get used to that name. Anyway, I want to make a confession. How do I do that?"

Amused, he asked, "Are you Catholic?"

"Nope. But doesn't God listen to everyone?" She pulled a lid off a large

rubber container, and he almost drooled at the cherry-covered cheesecake.

"Yes, He does. So, what's on your mind?"

She grabbed a knife from a drawer and started cutting a piece. "See, it's like this. My old man wasn't the best parent, and neither was my mom, but she's long gone, so that doesn't matter. Now, I've been trying the ole 'forgive and forget' thing, and most days, I do pretty good." Scooping the cheesecake onto a paper plate, she held it out to him with a plastic fork. "I need someone to test it for me. Now, where was I? Oh yeah, like, I'm trying to look after him, and he's trying to stay off the booze, but now there's Ty – that's our son, mine and Randy's – and my dad's all pissy because I won't bring Ty around to his place."

Joe took a bite, the cool, sweet cream bursting on his tongue. "Delicious. He hurt you, your dad." The thought made him sad for the girl and angry at her parents. Children were gifts to be treasured, never to be abused. "You can't trust him enough yet to risk your child. Commendable, and the right thing to do, so you can quit worrying."

"Really?" Her eyes lit up. "I'm not breaking the whole 'Honor thy father and mother' rule?"

"God works in mysterious ways. You're honoring your father by seeing he's cared for even though he didn't do the same for you while you were growing up. You're also showing him how a good parent is supposed to raise their child." He threw the empty plate and fork in the trash then laid his hand on her shoulder. "Go enjoy yourself. Today is for looking forward to the future, not for dwelling on the past. I won't be upset if there's a piece of that cheesecake left for later."

Father Joe spotted a small container with a piece of cheesecake in the refrigerator before coming out here, a note on top saying *For Father Joe & no one else.* The big rancher carrying around his six-month-old son kept a close eye on his wife, but Mickie flitted around, seemingly unaffected by the way he kept track of her. They weren't the only ones who exchanged looks that conveyed a special bond the likes of which he enjoyed with his priestly calling.

"Yes, Captain, I understand. I can't say I'm sorry, even if that's wrong. I'll tell Nick. Thanks for calling." A dark-haired woman came out of the house, her blue eyes startled to see him sitting there. She pocketed her phone, giving him a sheepish look. "Sorry. I didn't mean to interrupt you."

"You're not." He took in her pale face and sad eyes. "I'm Father Joe. Are you okay?"

She hesitated then shrugged, as if thinking *What the heck*? "I'm Melinda Walsh, and yes, I'm fine, just trying to assimilate how I feel about some news." She glanced toward the stables, and Joe figured she was seeking Nick, the ex-cop astride a large gray horse.

"If you're troubled, I'm a good listener," he offered. The poor woman appeared conflicted.

Melinda walked to the chair next to him and sat down. "It couldn't hurt to get your opinion before I talk to Nick. My phone call was from Nick's former police captain." She blew out a breath, her eyes staying on the other man who must mean a lot to her. "The man who murdered my father has died in prison. He only served a few months for what he did."

Joe nodded, now understanding. "And you think it's wrong not to feel bad for another person's death. We're only human, Ms. Walsh. God doesn't expect anything beyond our capabilities, which, in your case, would be finding compassion for a man who did such an awful thing. Believe it or not, you will find that kernel of empathy at a later date."

"You think so? I thought I was over my bitter anger with him, and my reaction of cold indifference took me by surprise." She fiddled with her ring finger on her left hand, but Joe couldn't detect any sign of wearing a ring there.

"Is there something else clouding your thinking?"

Melinda gave him a sharp look followed by a rueful grin. "You're as good at reading me as my Nick. Lisa, Poppy, and Skye think the world of you."

"And I of them." Joe rocked the baby, giving Patrick his finger to latch onto. Melinda would talk more or not; he let her decide.

After a few silent moments, she blurted, "He asked me to marry him." She pulled a ring out of her jeans pocket and held it up.

"And you're not sure you want to accept?"

"Oh no, I want to, more than anything. It's just that I don't want to make any more mistakes by jumping into something that sounds so right without giving it some thought. He feels differently." Melinda sought Nick out again, her hands balling into fists.

"Since you don't seem to mind my opinion, here's what I think. When it's right, it's right. It's that simple. I saw that with Shawn, and how he and Lisa got together so fast after a separation of twenty years. They embraced a connection that started as children and decided they had wasted enough time. Life's too short to waste on regrets, Melinda."

Jumping to her feet, she surprised him by leaning over and giving him a gentle hug, mindful of the baby. "You are so right, Father. Thank you." Straightening, she put the ring on her finger then wiggled it in front of him. "Congratulate me – I'm getting married!"

Joe chuckled as she dashed down the steps and raced across the yard. Nick dismounted when he saw her then caught her up in a hug, twirling her around to the cheers of several onlookers. This was turning out to be a fine day.

He searched the lawn for his boys, the three men who had come to him one night, abused and on the run. All those years after he'd sent them here, to Buck and Betty Cooper, he'd thought he'd done right by them. For the most part, he had. He'd been lucky enough to visit Buck shortly before his death of an unexpected heart attack a few years ago, and Buck told him how proud he was of the boys they both loved.

Lisa was sitting next to Betty, the young, traumatized girl who had also come to him that night, now a beautiful, secure woman who had captured Shawn's heart. Joe's only regret was keeping the two separated for so long. He thought that was best at the time – they were so young. They both had since assured him he'd done the right thing, that they could make it work between them because he'd given them the chance to find themselves first, before they connected again. He would never know for sure but was grateful for their assurances. His heart nearly burst with pride every time he saw them together now.

Joe rocked, his gaze seeking Dakota, the one he'd worried the most about. The path of revenge he'd taken upon leaving Phoenix had consumed him for years. His determination and hatred of the man who murdered his mother set him on a course toward destruction of this life, and the next. Joe had prayed daily for Dakota's peace of mind, and for him to find the one person who meant more to him than his revenge. Every time he saw him with Poppy, he sent up a prayer of gratitude. The feisty redhead had saved Dakota's life, her own issues giving him a new purpose in life. The man who had killed his mother – the one Dakota had walked away from seeking vengeance against to go to Poppy – had succumbed to the disease ravaging his body. When Dakota had taken the news with a nod and simple, terse statement of good riddance, a weight had been lifted from Father Joe's shoulders.

Clayton, his fair-haired, fun-loving boy, had surprised him the most when he'd settled down with Skye. He saved his ruthless streak for the courtroom, often, in Joe's opinion, forgetting compassion when he pushed judges for the harshest sentence without thought to other circumstances that might have contributed to a person's illegal behavior. But there he was, sitting with his arm draped over his talented wife's shoulders, laughing at something Betty said, his face reflecting nothing but love despite the fact Skye had come to him believing she'd committed murder. Like Dakota, he'd changed for the better for the right person.

Joe chuckled when Poppy nudged Jerry Sanders and her boss scowled at her. The taciturn sheep rancher hadn't mellowed much since taking up with Betty, but the fact he was here, socializing, spoke volumes about her influence. Joe was happy for her. Like him, she still grieved Buck's passing, but life did go on, and it was easier getting through the bumps and grinds with someone at your side helping you over them.

There were other couples he'd met, all

now happily married or just as happy, still looking for that one person to complete them. Neil amused Joe the most. The park ranger couldn't keep his eyes off the younger woman who flirted and teased with open abandonment Joe thought was cute. He could tell Neil wasn't sure what to make of her, or, more likely, what to do about how he felt about her. Oh well, they would work it out, just like all the others.

Little Patrick's gray eyes were drifting shut with a big yawn. Joe started to stand to carry him inside to his crib when he spotted his boys coming up the porch steps. Shawn came over and scooped the baby off his lap with a smile while Dakota and Clayton leaned against the rail and folded their arms.

"I'll go lay him down, Father. Listen to them." Shawn jerked his head at his friends then carried his son inside.

"What's on your mind, boys?"

Clayton rolled his eyes. "Will you ever quit calling us boys?"

"Probably not. This is nice." He waved an arm toward the guests.

"It's a nice place to live. Got plenty of

space around here," Dakota said.

"Yes, to both. What are you getting at?" he asked as Shawn came back out.

Shawn looked from his friends to Joe. "We want you to move here, with us." He pointed toward the woods. "There's plenty of room for a small house of your own, and we'd be close enough to help you, you know, as you get older."

Joe had trouble swallowing past the lump lodged in his throat. *My boys.* They might not be of his body, but he couldn't love them more. He cleared his throat, touched by the offer. "You do know the church will see to my needs."

"Not as well as we can. Besides, once the babies come, they'll limit our travel time to visit you," Clayton said.

"And you know you want to be around the kids," Shawn pointed out.

Joe turned his attention to Dakota, who remained quiet. "That area is closest to your place. What about your privacy?"

"What? You think I can't control my lust to give you and my wife the respect you deserve? We have the club for privacy," he stated with his usual bluntness.

Yes, me and Buck did right by these three.

"And, before you use our harsh winters as an excuse, we've already contacted your sister with our plan. She would love to have you stay in their mother-in-law suite during those months. That way, you can still spend quality time with your family in Phoenix and with us here. It's a win-win," Clayton argued.

Joe stood up, his eyes watery behind his glasses, but he could still make out each of their sincere faces. Seventy was fast approaching, and he couldn't think of a better way to enter the final stage of his life than right here with these fine men.

"A day doesn't go by when I don't thank God for the three of you. I think I'd like following in your footsteps and making my home here in Mountain Bend."

The End

About BJ Wane

I live in the Midwest with my husband and our Goldendoodle. I love dogs, enjoy spending time with my daughter, grandchildren, reading and working puzzles.

We have traveled extensively throughout the states, Canada and just once overseas, but I now much prefer being homebody.

I worked for a while writing articles for a local magazine but soon found my interest in writing for myself peaking.

My first book was strictly spanking erotica, but I slowly evolved to writing steamy romance with a touch of suspense. My favorite genre to read is suspense.

I love hearing from readers. Feel free to contact me at bjwane@cox.net with questions or comments.

Contact BJ Wane

My Website
www.bjwaneauthor.com

My E-mail
bjwane@cox.net

Facebook
www.www.facebook.com/bj.wane
www.facebook.com/BJWaneAuthor

Twitter
www.twitter.com/bj_wane

Instagram
www.instagram.com/bjwaneauthor

Goodreads
www.bit.ly/2S6Yg9F

Bookbub
www.bookbub.com/profile/bj-wane

More Books by BJ Wane

VIRGINIA BLUEBLOODS SERIES
Blindsided
Bind Me to You
Surrender to Me
Blackmailed
Bound by Two

MURDER ON MAGNOLIA ISLAND TRILOGY
Logan
Hunter
Ryder

MIAMI MASTERS SERIES
Bound and Saved
Master Me, Please
Mastering Her Fear
Bound to Submit
His to Master and Own
Theirs To Master

COWBOY DOMS SERIES
Submitting to the Rancher
Submitting to the Sheriff
Submitting to the Cowboy
Submitting to the Lawyer
Submitting to Two Doms
Submitting to the Cattleman
Submitting to the Doctor

COWBOY WOLF SERIES
Gavin (Book 1)
Cody (Book 2)
Drake (Book 3)

DOMS OF MOUNTAIN BEND
Protector (Book 1)
Avenger (Book 2)
Defender (Book 3)
Rescuer (Book 4)
Possessor (Book 5)
Redeemer (Book 6)

SINGLE TITLES
Claiming Mia
Masters of the Castle: Witness Protection Program
Dangerous Interference
Returning to Her Master
Her Master at Last

Made in the USA
Monee, IL
02 October 2022

15080749R00203